C000154767

Horizons II

Lance Clarke

Manor Cottage Books

i

First published by Manor Cottage Books and on ebook Kindle in November 2020.

The catalogue record for this book is available from the British Library

ISBN: 979-8-563254091

Cover design and typesetting: Lance Clarke

Cover image: Shutterstock – Man looking at Horizon

Acknowledgements

I want to acknowledge those who helped to proof read, edit, and encourage my craft: Jean Carrol, a good friend and Judith Leask, (Just Right Editing). I also learned a lot from the Oddfellows Hall Writing Group in Leamington Spa, led by Steve Calcutt an experienced tutor and literary agent.

Dedication

To my long-suffering partner Diane who listened patiently to endless versions of the stories and continues to be my critical muse.

Other books by Lance Clarke

Balkan Tears
30 Days
Not of Sound Mind
Cruel Harvest
Horizons I
Mary

Author's Comments

I love to write a story! Sometimes it comes from a playful exchange, such a tale told to me by my brother, which I turned into a written piece, St Thomas Christians, or Smoke and Mirrors, which I wrote after hearing at a party about the antics of a serial bigamist who told wild lies to at least three partners. The Dinner was spawned after a casual remark from a friend about a military dinner that was suffering from low attendance due to the advancing age its members. Scripts are all around us.

Life is full of interesting, funny, sad, or challenging situations. The little work I have done in supporting refugees gave me so many insights into their lives and a couple of stories reflect this. I hope the tales increase understanding.

We are all narrative creatures. We build up in our minds stories about what we believe is happening to us and why we win or lose. Hence the remark from a psychologist to an audience to always ask, 'what story did I tell myself', is not such bad advice!

Perhaps the secret is that life is what we make it – or at least, how we tell it!

Lance Clarke
November 2020

Contents

1

The Choice

So what? Why go back? We are free to cover the last few miles from Mosul to the advancing Kurdish fighters and will be safe at last. Safe from fear that pervades every aspect of our daily lives.

But Hajir isn't. Ahmed knows this too. We know what happens to Yazidi girls rounded up by ISIS fighters who have held the town for what seems a lifetime.

We stop. We stare at each other, our minds in joint communion, thoughts interlinked. Our heads say, *go,* hearts say, *return.* I look at Ahmed and he smiles ruefully. Wordlessly we turn back, making our way perilously through the rubble-strewn villages, past burned-out vehicles and the occasional decaying dead body left unburied. The air smells acrid. We can hear the Kurdish bullet and shellfire from behind us. They will not be long. It takes a full day to get back to Mosul and we eventually arrive at nightfall, exhausted but our nerves keep us alert. Few lights are on in the houses and streets, but there is a full moon that interferes with our wish to be invisible.

Silently, Ahmed guides me through the narrow alleyways to the shop where Hajir was left hiding in a hole behind a set of shelves. We gave her enough water and food for seven days with the intention of returning to collect her and run for safety only to later find that ISIS soldiers had set up a roadblock in the street immediately outside the shop. After waiting several hours, we could delay no longer and left with heavy hearts, uncertain of how long the soldiers would remain or when the predicted Kurdish attack on Mosul would begin.

To our joy, we see that the road outside the shop is now deserted. The building looks like a giant square skull, dark windows with mascara-like smoke smudges along the edges, and a double doorway with its cracked glass doors resembling a wide-toothed grin. After a short pause to assess safety of entry, Ahmed leads me, crouching and nervous, into the building. Our feet crunch on the plaster and shards of glass littering the ground. The sharp sounds echo around the room. Once our eyes are used to the darkness, we proceed quickly into the long corridors leading to a stockroom. Ahmed walks well ahead of me.

Without warning, a dark figure grabs him from behind, awkwardly pushing a rifle against his head. The figure looks left and right but does not see me as I move into the shadows behind them. He shouts at Ahmed, enjoying the creation of fear in his captive. I draw my small but razor-sharp hunting knife and advance noiselessly towards the two men. Shells explode in the streets, and he doesn't hear me above the blasts, and he shouts and digs his knees into Ahmed's rear.

Suddenly, it's all over. My knife finds his throat and the blood from his jugular vein gushes as he gurgles in death. The rifle fires a shot. He falls to the ground and Ahmed, and I stand absolutely still to be sure that there are no more ISIS fighters nearby. Luckily for us, ISIS men are always erratically firing shots in the air.

Ahmed turns and hugs me, relief in his eyes.

We move on, and soon we are with Hajir.

She puts her hands to her face and her eyes fill with tears, she tries to smile but her fourteen-year-old face is wreathed in fear. She is so young, so soft and so vulnerable. Ahmed gives her a map, a compass, and directions out of the city in case we get separated, and a bottle of water. He wraps his black scarf around his head and face. With his dark clothing, he looks like an ISIS fighter. Only a large silver clasp in the shape of a crescent moon holding the top of his shirt together assures me that it is Ahmed. He is braver than me. If needs be, he will walk amongst the enemy without fear. I simply cannot do that.

We move unseen from alley to alley. All is well, and we are close to the outskirts of the city. But it was too good to be true. Around a corner fifty metres ahead a Toyota truck, with six ISIS fighters on board, one of them manning a large machine gun, hurtles towards us. Ahmed and Hajir are ahead of me in the shadows of an adjacent street, but I am exposed in the crossroad.

I instantly know that I am doomed, and they must be saved. I raise the rifle I took from the dead soldier and fire it directly at the Toyota truck. The bullet hits the fighter manning the machine gun and there are shouts of anger. I run in the opposite direction to Ahmed and Hajir, as fast as I can, putting as much distance between us as possible. My heart is beating, but because my fear is for them, not me, it gives me superhuman strength. As I run, shells from the Kurdish bombardment begin to fall around me. I wonder who will take my life, ISIS, or the Kurds.

Shots ring out. I am hit in the ankle by a bullet and fall to the ground. I choose not to fire on my attackers, there are too many of them and resistance is pointless. When they reach me, they hit me with their rifles and bind me

3

tightly with rope. I am tied to the rear of the truck and slowly dragged through alleyways, the roadway surface ripping my clothes and tearing at my body.

I have read how torture strengthens resolve, but this is untrue. After being severely whipped, I would have given up my grandmother for respite or freedom. Twenty-four hours and many beatings later, my torturers are certain that my plea of "just wanting to leave" is sound. But I killed one of their soldiers and my fate is sealed.

Without time to gather my thoughts, I am half-led and half-dragged out to a small square around which there are fifty or so men and boys. The shouting and noise are deafening – so much hate. I look down and see that the block in front of me is stained with blood. The sun burns my face, and I am forced to kneel. Despite my situation, the fear and pain, I only care about one thing. As I focus my eyes, squinting at the baying crowd, I notice one figure standing immediately in my sightline and my heart leaps as I recognise the silver crescent moon at his throat. He catches my glance and absentmindedly raises his hand to his chest, and as he does so he curls his fingers, fist-like, and extends a thumb, then slowly backs into the throng.

She is safe! She is free! At this, I annoy my captors and laugh with relief. This wonderful feeling of satisfaction that Hajir will not suffer the awful fate of so many other Yazidis comforts my spirits, and I hardly hear the shouts. Fear still courses through my body, but is numbed by the wonderful, comforting news.

My head is yanked backwards, I see the sun and a I stare at the flashing knife raised above me, and I know that little Hajir will live to see that same sun and I give thanks.

2

St Thomas Christians

It was an itch that I just had to scratch. Here I was in Kerala, standing outside a hot and dusty railway platform, littered with cigarette butts and redundant lottery tickets, surrounded by a throng of people, hundreds of miles from my brother's house in Goa. It was during a night of curry and lots of beer that Bruce gleefully wove stories and descriptions about the work of St Thomas. The apostle left the middle east and travelled to Turkey and then India, preaching and establishing churches and communities along his route. They were harsh times for all religions.

The more Bruce spoke the more I became fascinated with the apostle's work. I wanted to know more about the local people who went on to follow Christianity for the centuries in this continent so riven with religious tension between Muslims and Hindus, and grudging toleration of minor religions.

I paid the driver and arranged to be collected from my hotel in two days for the return journey by road. Not for me the sweating torture of buses or trains on long hot and crowded journeys in India.

Bruce arranged for a local historian to meet me in the hotel. I booked myself in at reception and arranged for my bag to be taken to my room. As I turned, I saw a small man with a mass of grey hair and a voluminous beard, brushing crumbs from his white shirt and black trousers. He came over to me, smiled thinly and put his hands together in greeting.

"You must be Bruce's brother, Lawrence?"

"Correct, and you must be Ishwer?"

"You are also correct, my friend."

He shook my hand, and I felt the cold bones of his fingers with barely any flesh covering them. He had piercing grey eyes and seemed to be weighing me up. He tilted his head to one side.

"Come, let's eat some food and drink tea; you must be hungry after your long journey."

We left the hotel and although Ishwer limped badly, I was hard pressed to follow him as he weaved through the crowded streets. Eventually we settled at a small food stall and sat on wooden seats worn shiny by countless customers. There was a clattering of pans on stoves and loud chattering all around us. I wondered whether we would be able to hear each other. Almost immediately trays of thali, chapatis and glasses of tea were placed on the table in front of us. It was welcome and the variety of dishes from plain or creamy vegetables to the challenge of fiery curries teased my taste buds. When we finished, we quietly regarded each other.

"Your brother has a busy mind," said Ishwer, leaning towards me. "He wants to do and know everything, and I mean everything. We first met when he was trekking across India several years ago. His energy makes my head hurt."

We both agreed and laughed at Bruce's expense. I took on a more serious note and addressed my reason for coming to Kerala.

"Ishwer, I am here because Bruce told me that you knew things about the treatment of the St Thomas

Christians by the Portuguese when they first arrived centuries ago. I'm doing a thesis for my MA on International Relations. I believe that it's important that we understand how communities have behaved towards each other as times changed, but equally how some remained true to their religion or politics even under great stress."

Ishwer frowned deeply, the lines on his face resembling cracked mud. "It is just like him to entertain and at the same time inform those around him. Although there are things about this situation that can be explained rationally, they also have a haunting, pervasive presence in people's minds, no more so than here in Kerala. My friend, this can be dangerous. Bruce forgets that in his quest for information and jesting."

Intrigued, I asked him to continue. He drew in a deep breath and stared at me.

"It's quite simple. St Thomas did travel from the Middle East to India, and he set up communities and churches everywhere he went. They followed pure Christianity, as it was ordained from the very time of Christ. Love of mankind, no idols and no embellishment – pure and simple. Remember Christ's teachings? It was the very essence of life, giving people a structure to work and live within for the good of all those around them, and completely unselfish. It remained that way for this sect for generations."

He paused, frowned again, and swallowed his tea, by now quite cold.

"Then the Portuguese arrived. Bear in mind this was almost fifteen hundred years after the apostle St Thomas toured India, by which time European Christianity had been hijacked by kings, princes and, of course, the pope.

7

Idols had been created, saints invented, and stories made up to such an extent that the pure basic principles of Christianity were so shrouded as to be unrecognisable." He began to wring his hands and said in a faint voice. "They also brought the inquisition."

In my heart I knew what was coming, but said innocently, "My goodness. But they were all Christians, weren't they?"

Ishwer was silent for a while and then looked up at the ceiling. "Yes, and no. You see, as usual, politics was interwoven in European religion. The Catholic Church was used as the glue to subjugate the population and give strength to the Portuguese authority. No other religion was tolerated. Put simply, those who did not convert were tortured and burnt at the stake. A deal was eventually struck between the St Thomas Christians and the Portuguese, but the treatment of their communities and other sanctions put enormous strain on the relationship."

I thought for a while, the stresses in modern international relations between large economic powers and poorer countries reflected a similar problem.

"This area of Kerala is alive with diviners and mystics who claim to have powers to call up terrible memories. I'm not sure you should be asking such questions here."

I thought carefully about what he said, and hurriedly made notes. As I was preparing to get more information, I noticed a scruffily dressed unshaven young man with a rather manic look about him, as though he was extremely agitated, regarding me as he sat on a step across the road from the stall. He steadily held my gaze, then got up and walked towards me.

Ishwer looked alarmed and blurted, "Oh dear. This is wrong."

The young man reached me and grabbed my right arm, his fingers digging into my flesh. "Tell the world. Tell the world what they did to us. How they stole our gold and killed our people. Tell them." His voice took on a pathetic, fearful moan.

Ishwer got up and tried to release the man's grip but found it difficult. Two men got out of a small car nearby to join the fracas and gently prised the man's grip away from me. They spoke kindly but handled him firmly. The man's dress was ragged and dirty and his hair was uncombed, hanging in curls about his head. His eyes were wide and his expression fearful. He pressed his face into mine and I smelled strong garlic on his breath that made me recoil.

"Tell them, tell the world about what they did. They must be shamed."

The two men smiled politely, apologised, pulled him away from me and led him to their car.

Ishwer stood still, with a concerned look on his face. We watched them depart. I looked at him.

He shook his head and said resignedly, "I'll tell you because you have your brother's blood in you, and I know that you won't let this go! The young man is one of a number of people in Kerala who are possessed. They seem to have our history embedded in their DNA. You see, when the Portuguese arrived in 1510, they heard about the St Thomas Christians and sought to convert them to Catholicism. Their notion was that there was only one true faith and no room for any other. All others were heretics, simple as that. After a few decades of threats and rising tension, the Christian elders decided to send a delegation of men and women, headed by key religious figures, to the newly built Our Lady of the Rosary Church in Goa to meet with the head of the Catholic church. They would take gold and gifts to show their friendship, to remove any ideas that they were a threat. They were simple people and had no experience of religious intolerance, or malevolent politics, having developed good relations with ruling Hindus and Moslems for centuries."

He stroked his beard as he talked. "They were never heard of again. There were rumours, of course. You know how it is in times of stress. It was well known that the Jesuits had established a large centre of inquisition, to process heretics and bring them," he put on a sarcastic tone, "back into the true and one and only faith. But nobody knew exactly what happened. Legend has it that the delegation was never seen again – not a single trace.

It remains a haunting mystery that has been carried down through the generations in some families, torturing their minds. That young man is one of them."

"Surely the mystery can be solved."

"I am sure," Ishwer laughed and added in exasperation, "but only the Catholic hierarchy can give the answers that these tortured souls need."

"Then I'll go and ask them!"

He put his hands to his head, exclaiming, "Oh, my goodness me, you are so like your brother. The fire of injustice burns hot in his soul and yours too, I think. Go then, if you must, but you will get nothing." He thought for a moment, adding, "I don't want to feed the burning embers in your mind, but I must. You need to talk to Cardinal Falcow, in the Se Catedral de Santa Catarina, in Old Goa, where archives are kept. I will say nothing about him – you'll find out yourself."

Ishwer told me to relax and took me to three St Thomas Christian churches and other religious sites. He talked about how times had changed, and I knew that he was trying to deflect my thoughts from the turbulent early history to more modern times.

However, throughout the tour I could not rid myself of the need to find out what had happened to the delegation all those centuries ago. Strangely, but perhaps because I was so wound up with the injustice of it all, I got the feeling that I was being watched.

Back in Goa, my brother was amused, but registered a concerned expression when I told him of my plans, as though he had gone too far.

"Why don't you go to the Taj Mahal or Amritsar, learn some history, eat curry, enjoy the richness of this vast confusing country?" he said with faltering conviction.

I thanked him – but immediately arranged for a driver to take me to Old Goa.

After being dropped at a busy intersection by the cathedral, I walked across a badly maintained market square towards the large oak doors and entered. As I did so, a wiry chap with a mop of dark hair, dressed in what I took to be religious garb of a black robe with a chain and small wooden cross around his neck walked immediately in front of me. It was as though I was expected. He frowned and his eyes pierced mine.

"Hello, I wonder if I might speak to Cardinal Falcow. I want to learn more about the St Thomas Christians and wonder if there are records here in the cathedral archives."

He took a step backwards and held his hand up, looking over his shoulder as he did so. "Wait here," he said in a high-pitched voice.

He returned ten minutes later. "Follow me. The cardinal will see you now."

As we walked inside, a large bell rang, and I tried to get into conversation with my guide. He said, without looking at me, "That is the golden bell, so called because of its rich chime. It is the largest bell in Goa."

Interesting though it was, my mind was on other things. We walked into the cathedral, and I saw on either side of the large ornate altar, brightly coloured oil paintings depicting religious scenes. A massive font stood on the right and my earlier hurried research revealed that this was used to baptise converts after 1532. We entered a small doorway and climbed the stone stairs, finally reaching a large ancient timber door, studded with gold pegs. The guide knocked and a gravelly voice told us to enter.

In front of me sat a large corpulent man with a sweaty face held up by a large, flabby double chin. His religious robes hung around him as if attempting to disguise his shape. He did not smile. His bulbous eyes regarded me with an angry stare.

"What is this nonsense that you ask? You want to know about the St Thomas Christians. Why?"

"Cardinal Falcow, thank you for receiving me. My name is Lawrence Sinclair. I'm studying for a master's degree in International Relations. I firmly believe that we must a look over our shoulders at the trials and tribulations of religious and political groups throughout history and learn from events, especially in the face of schisms. For example, I understand that these local people worshipped Christianity in a very pure form, and I am curious to know how they were received by the newly arrived Portuguese catholic church, and indeed what actually happened to one of the delegations that came to Goa."

He glared at me without disguising his animosity.

"There is nothing to learn. You have been misled,' he waved his hands dismissively, 'some St Thomas Christians have risen to prominent positions in the Indian government over the years. So, you see they are neither persecuted, nor favoured. It is the way of modern India. How they were received hundreds of years ago is irrelevant."

He patronisingly splayed his hands wide, adding, "I suggest you look on Wikipedia." Then he cackled, letting his hands drop to the table with a thump.

I bridled at his manner and persisted. "But cardinal, in Kerala there is a lot of local history that tells of a delegation of St Thomas Christians coming to the first church consecrated here in Goa, to assure the hierarchy of their allegiance. It is said that they disappeared. I know that there was a Jesuit headquarters nearby and wanted to..."

The cardinal banged his fist on the table and the guide beside me flinched.

"Stop this nonsense now. These stories are no more than witchcraft, tales from people with deformed minds. Delegations did come to Goa and history tells us that we did our best to help them to convert to Catholicism – the pure religion, the one and only religion. We tolerated their heretical beliefs with patience – the fact that many persevered with their disgraceful worship and have endured to this day is a sad indictment of the liberal modern world for all things unworldly and evil."

His face was red and the veins on his neck stuck out – I could see them pulsing with his rage. I tried to speak but was prevented by his raised hand.

"Now get out and take your fake tourist interest in fairy stories with you. There is nothing for you to report to magazines or whatever your real purpose is – absolutely nothing. Make your filthy money by writing about something different. Go now, go." His voice reached a crescendo and I had no choice but to leave the office.

The guide took my arm gently and led me back to the staircase. On the way down, he suddenly stopped and pulled me into an alcove, looking about him and up the staircase. He whispered.

"You want to know the real story of the original visit of the St Thomas Christians to Old Goa to meet the Catholic leaders? Then listen carefully. They were taken to an old temple, commandeered by the Jesuits. I will say no more. Go to a teahouse at the other end of the town on Parliament Street. It is called the Green Leaf. Inside you must ask for either Om or Tarique and say that Naswar sent you. Explain what you want and after that you are in God's hands, my friend."

He stiffened and presumably for form's sake, returned to his officious posture, hurriedly leading me to the main entrance, theatrically pointing to the buses across the road. As I walked away, I looked over my shoulder and saw the scowling figure of Cardinal Falcow, framed by an arched window high above the main entrance.

It was not yet mid-day and I decided to go straight to the teahouse. I waved down a tuk-tuk and was driven through narrow cobbled streets, eventually arriving at a ramshackle establishment, with its sign – The Green Tea – hanging at a slight angle. Pleasant aromas greeted me as I entered, and I found a vacant wooden bench near the counter. Men sat at tables but, as ever, no women. A waiter approached and I asked for tea, adding, "I would like to meet with Om, or Tarique. Are they here today?"

The waiter smiled and moved his head from side to side, the amusing habit of many Indians.

"Why, yes, sir. They are over there." He pointed to two men deep in conversation by the window. They looked up and he waved them over. They approached warily. I stood and greeted them.

"Hello, my name is Lawrence Henslow. I am doing historical research about the St Thomas Christians. Naswar, a guide in the cathedral, advised me that you might be able to help me locate the original Jesuit buildings to which the Christians may have been taken."

The men shook my hand and looked at each other. They laughed uneasily.

"You are crazy. You want to visit that old temple and surrounding buildings? There is nothing but misery in that place."

"I will not be deterred." I said with undisguised conviction. "The world is a bad place already and I want to know just how bad it became for those people who visited from Kerala. Can you take me please?"

The older of the two men stroked his stubbled chin. "We are Hindu, so it matters not to us what you do. But if you want to persist with this nonsense, then take this liquid courage." He waved to the waiter in whose ear he whispered something that made him laugh. He quickly returned with a bottle.

"Okay, if you must. Give us three thousand rupees and one hundred more for this bottle and we will take you to the site. We will drop you there and after that you are on your own."

"What's in the bottle?"

"It's a spirit made from fermented fruits, very strong indeed. Drink it when you need courage – or should I say, because you will need courage!" They looked at each other and smirked.

"Tell me first about the site?"

"No, that's not a good idea. The site will tell you itself." He chuckled and shook his head from side to side. I

15

opened my wallet and paid up. I finished my tea, and we made our way outside and walked into the countryside.

We seemed to walk for ages, but it was probably only about an hour at a steady pace – my excitement was getting the better of me. Eventually, we stopped at a large clump of boulders overgrown by vines. I noticed that there was a small gap at one side.

"See that gap there," said Umwar, pointing a dirty finger to the right, "crawl inside and you will find that it runs alongside a rocky wall. Follow the path for about fifty yards and it will open up into the ruins of an old temple. It was this temple that the Jesuits used to...how shall we say? entertain their guests!"

The allusion of his words made my skin creep.

The men left, laughing as they went, and I crawled into the gap. I clutched my rucksack, which contained the spirit – I did not expect to need it. There were lot of cobwebs and I had to frequently stroke my face to keep them off. The light filtered through the vines and my imagination stirred as I heard noises in the undergrowth. As I brushed away the last of the vines, I saw the clearing and emerged into the sunlight, triumphantly, standing in front of a building made of large hewn stone blocks, with a domed roof. It was surprisingly undamaged. Alongside it, were the remains of square-shaped buildings, more European in design, each roof long since caved in and walls crumbled to half their size.

I scrambled towards what I took to be the temple; it must have been ancient even when the Jesuits arrived. Through the pillared entrance, I saw a circular hall, with an inner wall that contained doors that doubtless led to small rooms. I entered gingerly, my feet crunching small stones against the flagstone floor. My heart began to beat fast, and I decided to take a large swig of the spirit in the bottle. It burned my throat at first but strangely enticed me to drink more, and it became smoother to the taste. Unwisely, I took more swigs before putting in back in my pack. My head swam.

There was enough light for me to see a large circle in the middle of which was an oblong stone slab. I moved closer. I froze. To my horror I saw what looked like four iron bands, resembling manacles fixed into the rock, above which hung the unmistakable shape of a broken St Thomas Christian cross, recognisable by its four arms being the same size and the ends resembling lotus flowers. The significance was enough to convince me that this place had been used to break heretics. I sat back against the wall and pulled out my spirit bottle. Finding the place had been a success but did I really want to know more?

After more swigs of the spirit, I felt tired. It had been a long day. Despite my best efforts I could not stop myself from falling into a deep sleep.

I slowly awoke and realised that it was now dark. At least, I thought I was awake – my head was reeling from the effect of the spirit. As I sat against the wall, I became aware of the sweetest of sounds, musical chimes, and girls' voices, floating through the air. Then a parade of people in white gowns appeared around the circle, clinking small hand cymbals, and singing. They swayed and laughed magically, happy in each other's company. They held baskets overflowing with flowers, silks, and golden ornaments. An old man stepped forward and raised his hands to the sky as if calling upon the Almighty. The group circled the stone slab, and I could see a mist and smell incense.

All of a sudden, there were wild screams as figures burst into the room. They were dressed completely in black with masks across their mouths. On their chests were emblazoned bright white crosses. Their eyes glowed red in the candlelight. Beyond the door, outside, was a large bonfire that flickered yellow and orange against the black sky, with small sparks flitting around like fire flies.

The men and women were dragged, outside. They kicked and fought their tormentors, but they were no match for the stronger men. I looked on with horror as I saw them flung onto the burning wood, their plaintive, pleading screams turning to agonized moans as they were held in the flames by large poles wielded by the black-clad figures. Their demonic job done, they turned and came back into the temple. I felt sick. Inside, a young man lay manacled to the slab with a broken wooden cross above his head. A figure approached with a red-hot iron.

This was too much for me. I was incensed and screamed oaths in despair and anger and unsteadily rose from the ground. Two of the figures looked up and approached me. I had little coordination having just awoken from the effects of the spirit and they easily secured my wrists with coarse rope; I wriggled left and right to try and stop them. The rope scraped my flesh as they tightened it. I continued to curse and kick out at them. In the struggle the mask of one of the men slipped and I was startled to see that he looked just like a younger version of Cardinal Falcow.

"Bastard! You killed them. These innocent Christians. Why?"

"Heretics must die or convert," he screamed, and struck me across the face.

By now anger filled my body and adrenaline gave me the strength to fight back. I wrenched the rope from their hands and pushed them back towards the stone slab. The Falcow lookalike fell and hit his head, letting out a cry of rage. His companion angrily reached for me, and others joined in, leaving the young man on the stone, bent and fearful. As they approached me, I swung my pack at one of them who fell in front of the others, impeding them, and I ran for the entrance.

To my surprise, once outside, the sides of the doorway fell inwards and prevented the screaming figures from catching me. I turned towards the fire. I could see the sweet faces of young women in agony, reaching out of the flames towards me. The flames crackled noisily, licking the victims. In a frenzy I grabbed a pole and started to madly scrape large clumps of burning embers left and right. Then as the faces faded, lost in the glow, my eyes filled with tears.

I turned around and saw to my horror that the embers had set the surrounding undergrowth alight – I was now in the middle of a raging inferno. Fearful of being burned alive, I ran in the direction of the gap in the vines. I scrambled across the stony ground, branches cutting my face as I stooped. Eventually I made my way through the gap and along the wall to the road. I looked back and saw the whole area ablaze. As particles of hot red embers floated upwards in the sky, they appeared to take on the shape of a St Thomas Cross.

I was intending to find my way back into town, but the episode had been exhausting and I could go no further. I felt myself fainting and fell heavily to the ground.

I awoke face down on the dusty road the early morning sun warming my neck and to my great surprise found Ishwer standing over me. Relieved, I held out my hand.

"Oh dear, what a sight you are. What have you been up to?"

I looked at him plaintively, "How...?"

"I was so worried for you. It was easy enough to follow your tracks. I knew you would come to Old Goa. There are not too many white Europeans in this area and the tuk-tuk driver recognised your description. The men in The Green Tea told me of your mission and I enticed them to tell me what they had arranged with you. I chastised them severely. Here is your money back. I know too many policemen and the men readily conceded that they should not have led you here. As for the spirit, do not ever drink it again. It has hallucinogenic effects and can ruin your liver. You are safe now."

He waved and a passing tuk-tuk pulled up.

"I saw such terrible things. You don't understand. The bonfire, the Christians..."

"Poor boy. It was all a dream. A local farmer said that there was a fire, probably a small one behind those rocks, but he said it often happens on hot days. You are in bad shape, and tired. Come on now, get in."

I reluctantly got in the tuk-tuk. Perhaps he was right. I looked at my clothes and surprisingly they were in good shape, not at all suffering from burning embers or the scrapes of branches and rocks. I felt confused.

As we pulled away, I looked over my shoulder and saw, high on the hill above the boulders, a black-clad figure shaking his fist in my direction. I blinked and shook my head. When I looked back, it was gone.

I dozed and when we reached the centre of Old Goa, I chose not to return to my brother's house many miles away in Benaulim but booked into a hotel with Ishwer and went to bed. Had I been a fool? If I was, then sibling rivalry kept me from admitting it to my brother.

When I awoke the next day, I went for a shower. Had I been a drunken fool? Had I been taken for a ride by charlatans eager to take rupees from a gullible tourist? I was about to concede these points when the soapy water trickled down my body and stung my wrists. I looked down and recoiled at the sight of red lesions resembling rope burns.

The flight back to the UK was pleasant and I was feeling so much better after Ishwer encouraged me to spend a few weeks meditating at a local temple. I enjoyed a deep sense of calm. Looking back on the experience I am certain that rather than frightening me, it gave me a sense of purpose in my life. My thesis on the insidious effect of politics in religion on all aspects of society throughout history gained me an "A" grade, which pleased me.

My new friends are pleased too. I can never remember all their names but that does not seem to matter to them. They enrich my life. Their colourful costumes, chanting and beautiful singing brighten my cottage every day. There are so many of them always moving around my rooms, smiling and happy to be with me, as I am with them.

They bring me joy.

Tomorrow we will be placing a large St Thomas Christian cross above my garden patio - it should look nice.

3

Ten

One, two, three...up to ten. Count slowly - keep disciplined. Just ten and no more, count them and mark the spot, take up the count again tomorrow. It provides a prop for my survival; it allows me to pace myself, to keep to a steady focused routine, to survive.

I recall childhood days of warmth and brightness with friends, eating watermelons and giggling until our hearts beat fast. No multiples of ten in those heady young days, long before the chaos and seething hatred. Where there was light, not dark; fresh air, not stale stench; music and laughter, not silence. I continue with tens, adding beautiful memory markers along the way. You can't beat me. I am complete. I am whole. I am the centre of this tiny universe, controlling my actions and thoughts.

I started counting to ten when faces were pressed against mine, shouting obscenities, insulting my religion, my family, my sex, my person. I was confused and paralysed with fear. They were oblivious to my cries of innocence and with nothing to give them whatever, I had to withdraw or go mad; I withdrew. I parried every question with my new internal discipline: counting one, two, three, and up to ten, endlessly, slowly, and rhythmically like a mantra until the voices became insignificant and disappeared. One, two, three...again and again. Block them out, hear nothing, say nothing; nothing to say - keep on counting.

They cannot break me. In their determination they devise all manner of painful indignations to get information I do not have, never had, never will have, would never want. I use ten as my guide through the days of hell. I make this number my lodestone, its magnetism ephemeral and yet real, it points me in the right direction, and I obey this line and follow it without question.

All because of numbers. Nine / eleven - iconic shorthand that supposes to excuse a multitude of sins of fools, brushing aside rational thought or reason from victims. Let slip the dogs of war - cry havoc, cry pain, cry mercy, cry for vengeance, or cry for humanity. But then crying is useless. Surviving to tell the world the truth is my goal. To tell my story is to divide myself by two: my person and my religion. I understand the nine / eleven pain, but my ten keeps me sane to tell you that causing me pain is not the answer.

Then comes the final ten; it is almost over. One hundred days' solitary confinement, because of my failure to cooperate where cooperation is impossible. One hundred days of tens to kept me sane.

One, two, three...then the door bursts open and the light pierces my world hurting my eyes. Four, five, six...I hear voices, this time temperate, filled with a kind of resigned compassion as I stand before them, straight and defiant. Seven, eight, nine, my breath falters in my chest and my heart beats wildly.

I steadily walk towards the open door...Ten!

4

Smoke and Mirrors

I'm not really sure how it happened – I don't really care much, it just did. Do you remember how, in your anxious, sensitive adolescence there were times when you felt insecure and unsure of yourself? Well, I stumbled upon an idea to deal with this and deflect attention from myself by actually being someone else. Not physically, that would be impossible; what I mean is, to play a game of "pretend".

Let me explain. I might make a telephone call to a bank or building society with the aim of just talking, but in doing so I actually became someone else! I could be rude, well-mannered, funny, all sorts of personalities – it felt good. I was different from the spotty face that confronted me in the steamy shaving mirror each morning – I could form my alter ego the way I wanted, like a potter uses clay. I was in control.

The result was electrifying, and I would recommend it to anyone. After a while, I used this tactic less and less, and eventually consigned it to the bin. After school I went to work in a local car factory – not sparkling money, but enough for beer and takeaways. I joined a gym and managed to develop quite a good physique, if I say so myself. They say that if you've got it, flaunt it: so, I did. This was a good period in my life, time out with the lads and girlfriends along the way – but I wanted more.

I used to go up to London quite a bit and my favourite haunt was, The Coal Hole public house, on the Strand, where people such as Charles Darwin or Virginia Woolf, discussed politics, art, drama, and the finer things of life. The place was once the haunt of Edmund Keen, an actor, who set up the Woolf Room at the back of the premises It's every bit the old-fashioned London pub – mirrors, brass lights, antique tiles, dark wood fittings and a small balcony over which you could oversee the bar on the floor below. For me, it was my theatre stage, a place where I could conjure up all sorts of scenarios in which I was the central character. I would sometimes daydream that he asked me there to talk about the latest London plays.

It was in the Coal Hole that I met a gorgeous girl called Teri. She was fair-haired, had the most amazing figure and sparkling blue eyes. Her manner was slightly imperious, and this challenged me. She kept me at arm's length, and it seemed as though she was trying to judge my character. I wanted her, so I gave her just that, a character. I was, I said, a successful international freelance investigator. It was a complex and dangerous job to sort out cheats who defrauded insurance companies. Her face lit up like a torch and she turned her whole body to face me instead of standing slightly to one side. It was easy to insert one or two funny stories from my repertoire of ready wit – I have always been a bit of a raconteur. She laughed readily and to cement my newfound position in life I decided to order a bottle of champagne; having just sold my old banger I could afford to splash out.

I invented story after story, and how dewy-eyed she became as the tales unfolded. I told of seduction by rich businesswomen, of which, I opined, I was not proud. I described encountering dangerous managing directors who tried to have me killed and desperate men who would sell me their wives in order to get me to not deliver their bad deeds to the authorities; French, German, all sorts of nationalities crossed my path.

The months that followed were brilliant. I demanded that she respect my secrecy, no photographs, or chatting to her mates about my work. I had to protect my identity not only from future contacts, but from those I investigated. I think she began to feel part of my work, especially when I invented something that I felt needed female intuition that only she could help with. It was the was best tale I ever told; a fake dating agency preyed on girls who wanted a companion and took their money without fulfilling the deal. You know what? Teri actually worked out a damned good scam to set them up and catch them red-handed. I thanked her profusely and said that she should watch the newspapers for a result. She was well pleased - that night, so was I.

My low pay just about covered our nights out in posh hotels, but then living at home with my mum in Peckham meant that I had hardly any overheads to pay for. I hired a Mazda MX5 convertible, and we would go out for the day. I used the same dealer and car every time, so she thought it was mine.

I nearly dropped almighty clangers. After she saw me off at the underground station, I got off at the next stop and took the next train back to walk to the factory, when I bumped right into her. She had been buying a magazine and lost all sense of time. I had to think fast and said, with a cheeky smile, that I had lost my wallet. It worked, but only just. On another occasion, my tales grew a bit grand, and I said I was investigating the director of a London football club in a scam about ticket sales, only to find that her uncle worked at the same club. I later claimed that it had all been sorted out.

That was close.

After my Mum died, I sold the five-bedroom house and made a bomb. I rented a really cheap bed-sit just outside London within easy distance of work. When I wanted to see Teri, I hired the Mazda to pick her up and take her to a concert or perhaps a musical. Expensive, but then you only live once!

Like all good things, it became a bit routine. Gorgeous Teri, the good life, but a bit routine. Then along came Amanda. I met her in a Turkish restaurant along White Hart Lane after a Tottenham Hotspur match. She was the business, dark-haired, racy, and very loud, completely different from Teri. She fancied me from the moment we met – I was in thrall to her and felt out of my depth. So, I balanced the books, so to speak. I became a private detective. Well, how difficult is that? I read detective books and it was all in the stories, how they worked, what they did and so on. I made sure the same secrecy rules applied and thereafter seduction was a piece of cake.

It was worth all the reading to get my stories right, organising a different hotel for our lovemaking and of course, never using the Mazda. Worth it, that is, until Amanda and her brothers met me outside the factory gate.

You see, the problem with telling lies is that you have to get every detail right. Someone famous once said that he told the truth because he couldn't be bothered with having to remember what he had said previously. In my case, it was so true. She was a sharp cookie. I had given her a couple of stories, a bit over the top I suppose, involving Arabs, diamonds and the like. I was so full of myself, that although I noticed a strange frown on her face during one tale, I just went on and on, confident that I was untouchable. Frankly, I got some names mixed up and, well, I have to admit that the stories were terrible – over confidence, I suppose.

Her brothers, who resembled the Kray Twins, told me that she went into my jacket pocket and found Teri's telephone number in my mobile phone. Amanda called her and you can imagine how that ended.

Unfortunately, Amanda started to cry – brothers get upset when their little sister is hurt – and that raised the temperature to boiling point.

As I lay in the gutter, bleeding and spitting out a broken tooth, I swore that it would all end there and then. No more Billy Liar and no more spending money like water. That was it, I would change my life. I really meant it. The police visited me in hospital, and I maintained an absolute silence; identifying the brothers would only lead to more trouble or, worse, hilarity from everyone I knew at my situation. I kept schtum.

Well, you know how it is. After a big mistake, a feller decides to change based on common sense; but what do you know, events kind of gang up on you. The nurses were really sweet and gently tended my broken bones and bruises; they were all curious as to how it happened and felt really sorry for me.

It made me feel good. One day, my wounds were being dressed by a vision of loveliness, Carol, from Dublin, and we got to know each other very well. We dated, went for meals and have now been together for over a year, leading a modest, loving lifestyle, with the occasional exotic treat. She loves me to bits and hangs on my every word.

But then that's not surprising, not everybody gets to date an ex-special services secret agent – do they?

5

Crossing the Styx

The small island of Kastos in the Ionian Sea not far from the Greek island of Lefkada to the west and mainland to the east, was the perfect spot for Raymond Clarke. It nestled alongside another island, Kalamos, but was very much the little sister, with only one inhabited village, that being its port. Its size, at less than two and a half square miles, limited the population to about eighty people, and was only large enough to entertain tourists, mostly yachts. Raymond was content with this, and it meant that he could stay in almost complete solitude and yet observe just enough local life to cheer his depleted spirits whenever he ventured out occasionally, to eat in one of the four tavernas. He wanted to remain unnoticed and for the most part ignored.

However, the observant locals miss nothing. After two months they began to talk about him. He had taken a five-month lease of a secluded farmhouse near one of the two old windmills on the only island hill. Outsiders, usually artisans, writers or hippies had come and gone, comfortable in the warm sun, but unable to cope with the wet late autumn and dismal winter.

Raymond looked and sounded the quintessential Englishman. Although only in his mid-fifties, he dressed

29

soberly, no bright colours – all browns and beige. He suspected that the locals laughed behind their hands at the sight of his socks and plimsoles. His khaki shorts and white shirt made him look distinctly colonial and a battered straw hat completed the ensemble.

The locals found it odd that he arrived in late September, a time when most tourists are ending their sailing or hotel holidays in resorts on Lefkada island. They found him interesting to watch. and noticed that he was able to look after himself with ease and was a proficient fisherman, using a long rod off one of the beaches. He even traded one or two large fish for beer in the local tavernas. However, there was one thing about which everyone was in complete agreement: he looked decidedly sad.

One cloudy night, Georgios, a local fisherman, was drinking with his ribald and noisy friends in the Il Porto Taverna at the harbour. He was a broad man, with a tanned face, black hair, and bushy beard. He looked as though he could rip up the local mountain range with his bare hands. He and his friends fished all week and now it was time to drink. They always drank heavily on Fridays, each man receiving a free pass from a long-suffering wife, or girlfriend, on the basis that one night is better than every night.

"Hey, Georgios," shouted a skinny old man, whose cap had long since slid down the left side of his head so that it was supported only by an extremely large ear. "Did you leave fish for the rest of us?"

The others around him shouted raucously.

Georgios smiled and waved dismissively. "Why, what's the point? You boys can't catch your own grandmothers, let alone sea bream!"

A younger fair-haired man, dressed in long red shorts and a black T-shirt threw a place mat and it landed in Georgios's half-finished plate of kleftiko.

"You're too good for the rest of us, Georgios, you need a bigger challenge."

Georgios smiled through rows of impeccable white teeth. "And what challenge would test me enough, my college-educated young nephew? Shall I drain the Ionian or pull all the trees out with my teeth – what, eh?"

The group shouted and clapped, and the young man smiled good-naturedly at the put-down. Georgios was omnipresent, more than capable at all physical tasks in life. He was considered to be the village elder and knew all there was to know about the history of the island, as well as local mythology. His nephew considered him carefully. He wanted to give his uncle a substantial challenge, but what? Whilst his thoughts playfully raced through various ideas, he looked around the bar and saw Raymond sitting alone at a table, reading, occasionally sipping red wine, and eating warm saganaki cheese. That was it.

He nodded to his uncle. "Bring him to life then," he said. "He looks as though he could do with liberating from something, who knows what? Yes, liberate him, dear uncle and we will buy you wine for a whole night. What do you say to that challenge?"

The others egged him on, keen to see Georgios face something beyond just brute force. Georgios stroked his chin. Moments later he smiled broadly and stood up, rubbing his hands down his shirt, and flexing his enormous shoulders.

Raymond was aware of the commotion and that the group were regarding him strangely. He didn't care, in fact he didn't really care about anything. He was in bad odour with the few friends and distant relatives he had prior to leaving for Kastos. In fact, no one knew where he was, and he was happy about that. A book of crosswords and what remained of his enthusiasm for writing short stories was enough to sustain him. All he wanted was his world of written words, poetry, and fiction; how he wished that he could write his own life-script – but it was too late now.

He spiked a piece of cheese and sipped his wine.

Alcohol and bravado won the day. Georgios splayed his arms left and right and without a word walked towards the Englishman.

Raymond regarded the approaching Greek with amusement and detachment as the man-mountain headed in his direction.

Georgios reached his table, grinned, and said loudly, "Englishman, I am Georgios, and I would like to drink with you?"

Raymond carefully turned down the edge of a page he was reading and closed his book, placing it on the table. There was clearly no way he could avoid the offer. On the other hand, he really did not want company.

"Thank you, Georgios. My name is Raymond Clarke." He held out his hand and Georgios shook it hard. "I must tell you straight away, I really appreciate your kind offer, but I am quite happy in my own company."

Undaunted by this response, Georgios regarded it as a challenge. "That is not good my friend, everyone needs his fellow man."

He turned and yelled over his shoulder, "Hey, Yannis, another carafe of red wine over here, quickly." He sat down heavily on a chair that creaked in protest as it attempted to stand firm. "Sir, I mean, Raymond, if I may call you that. You are on our beautiful island, why do you want to be alone?"

"It's personal, Georgios. Don't think me rude, but for the moment at least I really am quite relaxed and, all things being equal, happy, and content to be on my own."

Georgios was a canny man. He regarded the loaded sentence carefully, opened his eyes wide and sighed theatrically. "You look sad, my friend and nobody should be sad on Kastos. You know, this island, together with Kalamos and Meganisi nearby, has seen much sadness, but look at us now."

He emphasised the point by slapping the middle of his chest with both hands, grinning some more.

The wine arrived and Raymond returned the smile; it was impossible not to, as Georgios' good nature was infectious. He raised a glass of cool red wine to his lips and after sipping it, said resignedly, "That's good for you all, Georgios. Thank you for your concern."

It was clear that Georgios had reached the limit of his introduction and was looking for inspiration. He was struggling for words. Despite wanting isolation and human nature being what it is, Raymond ended up helping Georgios out and regarded his new acquaintance with helpful interest.

"Georgios, I took time to study the history of the Ionian before I came here. You are certainly indomitable people. Over the centuries, you have been subject to rule by the Venetians, attacked by pirates and your islands sheltered refugee knights who rebelled against the Ottomans. That is fantastic history, my friend."

Georgios sat back and visibly glowed with pride.

Raymond continued. "I was surprised that control of your lands by an historically outdated family elite only ended in the last few decades when an international court freed you all from the tithe payments. You all persisted, you never gave up. You are really quite special."

Raymond congratulated himself and thought that he had nailed a place on the moral high ground that would allow him to gradually exit Georgios' company without ill will.

Georgios' face lit up and hew spoke with enthusiasm. "Yes, Raymond, that is what I tell my children and my grandchildren."

There was a strange silence between them, and it became obvious that Georgios was not going to give in.

"You are good with words my friend, but I came here to talk about you."

Raymond sighed inwardly.

"There's not much to talk about I assure you. Okay, look, I am perhaps a little sad, but sadness is selfish, it seems to always bother others more than the person suffering. So, let's drink some more wine and have nothing of it?"

For the remainder of the evening, fuelled by more carafes of red wine, they talked politics, history, football and strayed once or twice into Georgios' family background. It was past two o'clock in the morning and Georgios's friends had long since left the taverna.

Georgios stood up unsteadily and took Raymond's hand. "Listen to me, my friend. I want to show you something special. It is the church of Agios Ioannis Prodromos, near the harbour. I know the priest and he will give you access. When you enter, your eyes will take in the most beautiful majesty of the interior and you will instantly be happy, I promise you."

Protesting and thinking at the same time, is a challenge especially with a belly full of red wine, and it failed, as Georgios used the ancient tactic of feigning insult should Raymond even consider turning him down - the deal was done. They arranged to meet in the town square at ten o'clock in the morning.

Raymond tossed and turned that night and wrestled with his thoughts. On the one hand, it was kind of Georgios and actually pleasant to be so forcibly befriended; on the other, he knew it was inevitable that he would make him sad.

The next day was as bright as ever and the temperature a pleasant twenty degrees Celsius. There was the hint of a mist over the sea and a distinct feel of approaching autumn. The rainy November days would arrive in the next few weeks, but for now, Kastos clung to the last of the warm sunshine. It was a long walk to the town square, which fronted the church, and he arrived to see Georgios already there, waving happily to attract his attention. The large oak door was wide open. He realised that he had not given the prospect of viewing the decor much thought.

As they entered the church, Raymond felt the cool air gently brush his face and the smell of incense enveloped his senses. Slowly, his eyes adjusted to the dim light. He was overwhelmed and he felt as though his mind was being emptied of negative thoughts. It was all quite beautiful, just as Georgios had promised. The oil paintings on the wall showed biblical scenes, the colours filled his senses with joy and all he could do was stand and stare.

Georgios leaned towards him, smiling broadly, and was quite clearly pleased. "They are the work of a celebrated local artist Spyridon Gazis. I know him – he is a friend of mine."

Large screens painted in gentle pastel shades stood to the left of the altar, which was adorned with silks of deep colours. Raymond could hardly speak and felt incredibly at ease as he walked very slowly and silently around the interior. Georgios looked at him with obvious delight.

After almost thirty minutes they left the church and walked to a centuries-old olive tree nearby and sat in the shade on a wooden seat that encircled it.

"So, my English friend, you see, Kastos is no place for sadness?"

Raymond closed his eyes and put his hands to his temple, finally resting them on his lap, before turning to Georgios. He looked straight at him and addressed him in a kindly.

"Georgios, thank you so very much. The church was incredibly beautiful, and I can tell you that I am indeed far happier than when I went in." He faltered slightly. "I must tell you something. I will remember this place for all the time that I have left. That is to say, more accurately, nine months at most. You see," he paused for a moment, "I have cancer."

Georgios' face contorted. After a minute or two, he blurted, "It is true?"

"Yes, old chum, it's true. Please don't let that make you unhappy. I mean that, I really do. I am quite resigned to my death. I have had a great life, but along the way I never married or made friends, so the unhappiness I leave behind me is almost negligible. There is only a handful of people to grieve for me."

"You are to die then?" Georgios repeated, his face now resembling crumpled brown paper.

"Oh dear. Don't be upset. Be content that this beautiful church has really been very special for me. It has been a wonderful experience, thank you so much for sharing it with me."

He put his hands on the Greek's sturdy shoulders to steady him.

To Raymond's alarm, Georgios let out a howl and put his hands to his face to stem tears that now flowed freely. He was nonplussed at the outburst from a man he hardly knew. Eventually, the tears stopped, and Georgios regarded Raymond gravely. After a few minutes, he spoke in a quivering voice.

"My wife, Anna, died suddenly two years ago. Raymond, I never had time to say goodbye, or talk about the things people talk about in such circumstances. I wanted to tell her how sorry I was for being, well, loud and sometimes stupid. She never knew how much I loved her."

Raymond's thoughts about his own situation faded quickly into the background and he focused on Georgios. "I'm sure she knew," he said gently

"But I don't *know* whether she knew it. I don't *know* for sure," said Georgios, who was agitated and self-absorbed, fidgeting and looking around him but not directly at Raymond.

Georgios put his hands to his head, rubbing his dark scalp and walked away. Suddenly, he turned as if inspired and sat down again, and said abruptly. "You can help me, my friend."

Raymond was startled. "Er, how, Georgios?"

"When you are in heaven, you will see my Anna, yes, that's it. Tell her about me and how successful I have become. The type of man I am and how much I really loved her, especially that." He got even more excited, and the words spilled out of his mouth. "Oh, and that her eldest grandchild has got a place at university in Athens, that's important too."

Details of more family events and successes followed in a torrent of sentences, as if there was a time limit on his speaking. It was now all so jumbled and yet matter of fact.

Raymond's situation was now completely out of sight. If Georgios had not been so upset, Raymond would have seen a funny side to the unfolding scene.

A moment or two passed, then Georgios, as if suddenly remembering he'd left a pan on a hot stove, quickly stood up and addressed Raymond in an urgent tone, hopping from foot to foot.

"She will need to know you are coming! Oh yes, and you must also ensure that the ferryman, Charon, takes you across the Rivers Acheron and Styx that divide the world of the living from that of the dead. Oh, and Raymond, if you do not pay him, then you will be forced to forever with the restless souls in Hades. You don't want that my friend," he said earnestly, "You must take silver, to pay Charon. When you get to heaven you must talk to Anna for me."

As if in another world, Georgios began to sort out the arrangements for the preparation and journey. He was oblivious to Raymond's look of disbelief, utterly busy in his own thoughts, muttering to himself and pacing up and down.

Raymond didn't know what to say. He tried to gently talk rationally to Georgios, but there was no turning his mind. The mixture of resurrected grief, folklore and myth was too strong a cocktail. To his surprise he realised that he didn't really mind. Why should he after all? They parted and Raymond promised to do his best. For his part, Georgios went in search of a medium to call up his late wife's spirit to let her know what was coming and the priest to pray for her soul.

Raymond walked back to his farmhouse, shaking his head with disbelief. It was only when he was fishing from the quayside later that he suddenly burst into uncontrollable laughter. He was happy. Neither of them had spent even a second talking about his imminent demise and that diversion suited him very well. More importantly, he was left with the uplifting thought that his death would give a decent grieving man some kind of closure, whatever form that might take.

When he finally stopped chuckling, there was tug at his line and he reeled in a huge sea bream – result!

At a quiet tree-lined cemetery near Bracknell in Berkshire, a vicar gently placed a small varnished wooden casket of ashes onto two small canvas straps above a shallow hole, its edges lined with green plastic grass. He said prayers and one of the two mourners, a neighbour of Raymond's, stepped forward and muttered a few words, contriving recognition of his good character and sense of humour.

Before the vicar lowered the casket into the ground, a swarthy, bearded man came forward and, as had been previously agreed, was allowed to open the casket an inch or two. He then placed two silver coins inside, stood back and bowed his head.

Raymond's journey across the Styx to avoid the dark underworld was ensured.

6

It Was Just Business

I don't normally get emotionally connected; it doesn't do, don't you see? But he was different. Of course, I've had assignments that involved a variety of people, from the good and honourable to the bad and despicable. It never made any difference to me whatsoever – it was all just business, simple as that.

Jim was different. I hate to admit it, but he was. We first met, by appointment, in a quiet bar in Detroit near the busy train station. He impressed me with his simple logic and selfless attitude to the business to be undertaken; it was unusual. Although grey-haired, his physique was sporty and he had blue-grey eyes that stared straight at me, full of determination and incredible fortitude. He was clear-headed and extremely focused. He had been through a tough time. His wife had recently left him and taken the children with her. From what I have seen over the years, one or the other of the parties suffers – in his case he took the biggest hit. Anyway, he eventually found someone else, and a candle was lit again; his life started anew, and he was allowed a brief glimpse of happiness. I say brief because he was now forced to do business with me.

I was a poor substitute as a counsellor. In fact, I did none of that at all – it's simply not what I do. I create misery. I don't help to repair it. I deftly avoided discussion about his personal life. But the basis of the business rested on some aspects of it, so I had no choice but to listen. In the end I quite admired him. That's the Godamned truth of it.

So now I find myself four years later standing on the shores of Lake Tahoe, Northern California with Jim, looking across the shimmering water that reflected the light of the moon straight across the surface to where we stood. We said little. I let time go by slowly – I was in no hurry. We could get down to business soon enough, although the full details had by now eluded Jim. When we did talk, he apologised all the time for this and that. He smiled constantly and I found that irritating. I reminded him that he came by taxi, and this stopped him continuously fumbling for his car keys. I changed tack and tried to talk football and baseball. To my complete surprise this had the effect of instant recall, and he cited the names of kickers, fielders and much more. It was amazing. Then he asked me where we were; I told him – again.

I started to feel really sorry for him. That's an absolutely dumb thing to do in my business, I know, but I did. I liked him. I felt sorry for his partner too. All those years ago when we sat in that bar in Detroit, he had described her as loving, supportive, and pragmatic, given his situation. She was, a brave partner in all the business pre-planning and the key player, especially regarding the end game and also, I'm sorry to say, the payment.

We walked further on to the edge of the lake and Jim seemed completely lost in his thoughts. Then, would you believe it – me, of all people – I actually re-buttoned his jacket because he had gotten the sequence wrong and it looked stupid, one side lower than the other.

He stared at me as we stood by the water and I knew he was searching for my name, so I told him. I knew he would ask again. Suddenly, my mobile phone rang, and this made him visibly jump with fright, the gentle but vacant smile on his face an indication of surprise.

I read the text: 'Okay. It's time now.'

Jim was quite calm and relaxed, looking out to the middle of the lake, when I put the cold barrel of the revolver just behind his neck, at the base of his skull. It was the right spot. He died instantly. I caught his body before it fell and lowered him respectfully towards the ground. I put his arms across his chest and straightened his clothes. Unaccountably, I found myself standing straight with my hands held in front of me, looking down on him, as if in prayerful thought.

I jerked myself back to reality – what a schmuck – and shook my head and briskly walked away.

It was after all, just business, that's all – just business.

7

The Game

Adnan lay in the wet shrubs that carpeted the forest outside the village of Subotica in Serbia. It was cold and his anorak had long since lost its waterproofing. He kept quite still, even though his ankle throbbed, and his hands were sore with cuts from razor wire. Raising his head a little, he saw torch beams flashing in wide arcs, like warriors' swords in a Star Wars movie. The thought of getting caught made him shiver. He definitely did not want to be sent to a refugee camp where he would be registered, to spend his time waiting endlessly in the squeaky-clean palace of boredom for a visa to leave for Northern Europe. His friend Sami said that though the place was warm and safe, it was a slow way to lose your mind.

Sami joined Adnan and the rough sleepers sheltering as best they could in the forests. "Are you okay?" he whispered, "I thought I'd lost you."

"Yes, all good. Sore, but all good."

After an hour, the cold and wet was too much even for the torch-beam policemen and they left the area, taking with them a group of bedraggled young men who looked weary and resentful.

Adnan idly kicked a tuft of grass and dolefully looked at Sami. "They got Kasim and Haidar."

Kasim had been a student and Haidar a trainee doctor in Iraq and had formed a strong friendship with Adnan. They had a lot in common: music, sport, and a love for reading. There were no books in this dank place. Adnan would miss their lively and entertaining discussions. Despite their disappointments, they trudged wearily back to a derelict smoke-stained building used as a safe haven. They accepted the daily trials. Resignation and cautious optimism were the balm against hopelessness. When you've travelled thousands of miles already to get a foothold in Europe, there is no quitting at the last few hurdles.

Adnan put his arm above his head, stretched his muscular body, then ran his hands through his dark hair. He said ruefully, "Oh well, more rice and meat from the BelgrAid charity again tomorrow. I'm so hungry. I am grateful, but I thought I might one day offer to show them how to prepare kibbeh and tabbouleh, what say to that?"

Sami laughed. "You live in dreams, my friend. But I'm glad to be with you so I can share them. For now, I'm exhausted and wet, and just want to rest.

They reached their haven and settled near a smelly fire spitting as it tried to cope with the wet wood and other rubbish. They wrapped themselves into damp sleeping bags that nevertheless provided some warmth. Sami treated Adnan's cut hands and afterwards sleep came quickly to them both.

The next day they breakfasted on potato crisps and water. Adnan looked out of a frameless window at the clearing in the forest and the bodies of rough sleepers, hunched against the drizzle. Wispy yellow smoke from the bonfires, a little thicker than the morning mist, hung low on the ground. November is a cruel month for rough sleepers. At mid-morning, a charity truck driven by foreign volunteers delivered food, clothes, and footwear. Adnan noticed that this act of kindness from strangers was received with good manners by the sleepers, who crowded around the vehicle smiling and giving thanks.

The sleepers were almost all males; they shared a common rite of passage: the chance to get undetected onto a train or truck and seek a new life in a safer land. Adnan knew well enough that the odds were stacked against them, yet there was a sanguine expectation that as long as traffic flowed, they all had a chance.

The charity truck was about to depart when a black Serbian police vehicle stopped at the junction fifty metres away from the building. Tensions rose, the previous day a large threatening group of locals had gathered in the roadway shouting insults urging the sleepers to 'go home' and the police simply looked on. The policemen now got out and stood observing the derelict building. They looked menacing, arms crossed, their belts holding pistols and batons. Hurrying to the junction, the charity truck stopped, and two volunteers got out and talked cheerfully to the policemen.

The boys eyed the police warily, ready to run. A uniform often meant trouble at home. Nothing changes. It would be different in Germany or the UK – they knew that. After a brief exchange and handing over of what looked like a few pairs of new boots, the policemen left, and the sleepers breathed a sigh of relief. That was all the volunteers could do. Adnan remembered the charity leader's words: *We can't help you swim, but we can stop you from drowning!*

Adnan noticed Sami's weary expression and slapped his arm, saying encouragingly, "Faith, brother, faith. They're gone. And tonight, we try again. Tonight, we will be successful, you'll see."

"Again, and again," said Sami looking down at his feet. "Why do we do it?"

Adnan put his arm around his friend's thin shoulders.

"It's a throw of the dice, my friend. You know that. There is just a chance that we can get through the border. My family sold everything they had in Syria to send me to Europe. I must honour them by trying my best." He pointed across the clearing. "See Yazdan, from Kabul, over there by the water barrel. He was a teacher and the Taliban made threats on his life. His parents also gave him money to go. We are all indebted to loving families. Our aspirations are their dreams."

They parted, touching clenched fists, and said no more. They knew better than to trespass on the thoughts of others. From friendship grew strength; it welded them all together and gave them a sense of purpose. The sleepers would meet and compare successes and failures, dreams, and aspirations, and share experiences to improve their skills to play, *The Game.*

That night the sunset was bright, right to the last moment as the golden ball dipped below the horizon. This was not what they wanted. They needed complete darkness, as they crept towards a large truck park where vehicles had already been checked and cleared at the Hungarian border. The park was surrounded by wire fences and lit by arc lamps and police patrolled the perimeter. Thankfully, there were no dogs. Dogs were unpredictable and dangerous – they had a tendency not to listen to reason.

Early evening was a good time to make a dash for a truck, because the truck drivers showered and then ate in one of the canteens, before driving off. Unfortunately, the sleepers arrived later than planned and they had to be quick.

A three-man police patrol walked along the wire fence and stopped briefly to light cigarettes. They moved on. When they were far enough away, the whole shrub land seemed to come alive and crept as one towards the wire fence. Several shapes moved to the fence and began cutting holes big enough to crawl through. They stopped to look out for more guards. There were none.

One by one, shrub camouflage was discarded, and the sleepers crawled through the fence; there were dozens of them, and they quickly ran towards the trucks and trailers. Inevitably, security cameras spotted them, and an alarm sounded. Adnan and Sami headed for a truck with UK plates. The security cables surrounding the tarpaulin were difficult to release and it took too long. Adnan took a large metal bar from his pack, dug it under the lip of one of the hooks and leant all his weight on it and after considerable effort it eventually gave way. He then dealt with two more. Finally, a gap was created, but it was only big enough for one slim person to get inside. Adnan's earlier confidence ebbed away, and he turned and to Sami, who looked helpless and beaten.

Without a second thought, Adnan grabbed Sami and pushed his head under the tarpaulin, then forced his friend's thin body inside the truck.

The police were getting closer and would soon be upon them. Adnan smiled resignedly. He calmly reattached the security cables surrounding the tarpaulin so that they looked untouched and then stood as if about to try and undo them. As the police approached him, he feigned helplessness with the cables, theatrically threw away the metal bar and ran towards the perimeter. The police focused on him and not the truck, shouting and chasing him. When they caught him, he raised his hands in a gesture of surrender.

These policemen were friendly, and merely escorted him back to the control room. He was grateful, but still shaking; his last two escapades had resulted in severe beatings.

Stunned by his friend's sacrifice, Sami crawled deeper into the recesses of the truck, squeezing around boxes until he found space big enough in the centre of the cargo. He had two small bottles of water, some bread, and a bag of raisins. Half of him wanted a long uninterrupted journey because it meant that he was successfully dodging the customs checkpoints. The other half of him did not look forward to the diet and hygiene discomforts, for which he carried tissues and small plastic bags.

Back in the police post, Adnan could only gaze out of the window at the UK trucks as they joined a line of vehicles and moved slowly in convoy over the border. He sighed heavily. If escape cannot come to you then the best feeling in the world is to help someone else. He knew that he would be processed and taken to a refugee camp. There he would behave himself for a while and later abscond to try again. He would never give up his quest to find a better life for himself.

Adnan said a prayer for Sami, his faith comforting him. He would continue to play, The Game.

8

Look at Ron

How things change. So quickly, or perhaps not – it just seems that way. Ron had tightened the grubby collar of his quilted jacket and put another piece of cardboard under his bottom to keep out the cold. The paper cup at his feet contained a few coins and could pay for a hot coffee later.

What a privileged career he had enjoyed. A successful architect, Ron had commanded a high salary. It paid for a good house in Surrey and private school education for his girls. His wife Eleanor enjoyed frequent city breaks and a substantial allowance, as well as membership to a prestigious lawn tennis club. Life could not have been better. Then it all changed.

Ron was popular within Swinton's Architects in Central London, but the financial crash of 2008 slowed the economy such that the company had to lay off staff due to a lack of orders. It was the highly paid architects that were at risk; younger people were affordable. There are no loyalties in business when the stakes are high. Ron was made redundant. The shock was enormous. Other architect companies were also feeling the effects of recession and there was simply no work available. Ron knew nothing else. He held out for a new position for too long - far too long.

The effect on home life was catastrophic. Family tensions ran high. Eleanor was supportive at first, but when the redundancy cash ran out, so did hope. They argued over small things and often spent the evenings in complete silence. The children left private school and were sent to grandparents, and Eleanor got a job.

Ron made a fatal error: he started drinking to solve his depression. He knew that alcohol, in moderation strengthens personal reserve, but it also weakens the already weak, giving them false sanctuary in oblivion. In oblivion you don't have to talk to anyone. Isolation replaced teamwork, scowls replaced smiles and silence overtook discussion. The atmosphere was as taut as a piano wire, tightened but not played. Divorce was inevitable.

The divorce settlement was fair, and he could have kept half the value of the house. But it would have meant a loss for his family, and he felt that he had contributed enough to their misery. He did the only thing he could. He simply walked out, rucksack on his shoulder and a few quid in his pocket. The streets of London became his home, oddly enough, his sanctuary. Although he was dependent upon charitable acts of kindness, there was no pressure. He met amazing people many of whom were in the same position as he was, there was camaraderie and support from those he would not even have stopped to talk to a year earlier. It was strange that at this time in his life, under such circumstances, he should see the true values of human nature.

Now, there was no sadness and no regrets – it was all long gone. The debilitating feeling of failure, the imposter that gives false label to those to whom events in which they had no hand, was now no more. He was no longer a failed architect, or a failed husband – he was nothing. Ron's face was splattered with rain that lazily dribbled over his rheumy eyes, grey and staring.

In the shadow of a faded shop doorway a scruffy young man with sallow features and long greasy hair, partially hidden by his hoodie, lounged against the wall. He took a drag from a thin roll-up cigarette cupped in his hand and blew smoke towards Ron's silent form. He eyed the coins in the cup. He waited, looked left and right and then darted forward, athletically bending low to scoop up the cup in one swift move. He gave the hunched form no more than a perfunctory glance.

However, that brief glance stuck to him like glue. Barely four metres away, he stopped in his tracks as if not fully in charge of himself. Turning his head slowly he looked at Ron then to the cup, and back to Ron. He put his hand to his head and saw his reflection in a large puddle and let out a low moan as if not liking what he saw. Looking up he saw the figure of a policeman walk along a concourse not far away, and raised his arm, calling loudly for help.

Minutes later the policeman arrived and pronounced Ron dead. The young man clutched the paper cup tightly and stood silent whilst an ambulance was called. He looked dejectedly at the few coins in the cup then slowly walked to a nearby street collector and deposited them in the tin.

Ron's last act in life was to give to charity.

9

Poor Jack

An eerie sky hung over what remains of the village of Beaurair in the department of Hauts-de-France. It was enveloped in mist spread far, clinging to the hills, creeping over them like spilled milk. The setting sun tried to break through, intermittently flashing shards of light on the land below. The coldness of the clouds caressed the warm land and low rumbles of thunder could be heard as the air became alive with static. It was a time for sensible people to stay indoors.

The yellow twilight came and went, stroking the plastered walls of a cottage on the highest hill, three miles from the village. Nothing stirred save the banging of a loose window shutter moving in the gentle breeze.

At the corner of the cottage a hazy, wispy form lingered. It was of a WWI British soldier dressed in a long greatcoat bearing two stripes. He was wearing a battered hat and binoculars hung around his neck. His face was careworn, and he looked distressed. He moved erratically around the outside of the house, looking in the windows and occasionally away and over the valley. He seemed to move through obstacles rather than around them. Eventually, agitated, he reached the front door and stood staring at the it for some time. He reached for the handle and turned it. The door opened and he slowly entered.

Inside, the room swirled in a kind of vortex around him. Lights and sounds of artillery barrages, and the sharp crack of rifle shots rang out. The clatter of marching boots came and went, as did the voice of Marie Lloyd, the famous music hall singer, singing *Now You've Got Your Khaki On*. There was ribald laughter, soldiers shouting waggishly, "...Ello, Sergeant Major, d'you love me...?" and the unmistakable clink of beer glasses. The sounds slowly died away and the room took on a brighter, but dishevelled look.

The wraith put his hands to his head and stared at three men dressed in British First World War uniforms, asleep on a couch and chair.

In the corner of the farmhouse by a window stood Corporal Jack Apsley, smartly dressed, ramrod straight, looking through his binoculars at a blood-red sky and the valley below.

"Call to arms, boys, for King and country! Look at this view – what a vantage point. I'll tell yer, now we're unloaded and set up here, the bleedin' Krauts won't get into this valley without me noticing and letting Captain Andison know on that field telephone."

He pointed to an oblong olive-green tin box with wires sticking out of it by the windowsill. "I mean it, I do, y'know. I'd tell General Haig if he was here, it's my duty!"

The soldiers began to stir, and an infantryman looked at him from the blanket covered couch and said sarcastically, "Well done, *corporal*," rolling the word slowly out of his mouth, and looking at the other two who were now stirring, "we'll beat the enemy for you and the King, that we will. What are you doing anyway, aren't you knackered like the rest of us?"

"I'm doing my job, soldier. A frequent recce of the hillside. Just like I've been doing for the last four days. This is the best site ever."

The soldier sniffed. "And what do you see my esteemed *corporal?*"

Jack turned abruptly and addressed him in a school-masterly tone.

"The valley is the perfect to observe any advancing Krauts, stupid soldier. In the last ten days we've been pushed back from St Quentin to Amiens; blimey that's fifty miles the Fifth Army has retreated. It was a bloody rout, that's what it was. The Somme area has to be held and that's all there is to it. Our job is to keep watching for enemy movements and if we see them, pass sightings to our guns over the ridge. Simple, see! Even a dork like you can understand that."

"And for that we should be eternally grateful, *corporal.*"

Jack's face reddened with anger.

"When are you going to count your blessings, ungrateful prat? Only ten days ago we were up to our bollocks in freezing water and rats in a stinking trench. Now we are in this warm dry palace, you're a pain in the arse. This is an important duty and don't you bleeding forget it!"

Another soldier on the sofa who was rubbing his eyes and adjusting his webbing belt, which had ridden up his body, made to calm the situation. "He's right, Harry, give it a rest, will you? Before that I spent six months with green rookies just out from Blighty. It was sheer hell. They were paranoid about rumours that the Krauts were tunnelling under the barracks. It was fed to them by an old-timer as a joke. Anyway, the stupid buggers would wake up during the night at any sound and start prodding the ground with their bayonets."

"Nice one, Andy," said Jack, grateful for a humorous intervention.

Harry remained sarcastic and looked from Andy, back to the Jack, "Well, *corporal*, I am chastised, that I am. Forgive me. Perhaps it's because I see this as an exercise to show the high and mighty how good you are, what with you being Royal Artillery...sorry, a *bloody gunner,* to use army vernacular. Don't worry, we infantrymen are used to propping up the rest of the army. We'll make you look good, *corporal.*"

Jack straightened up and walked towards the couch. "Not so, and you bloody know it. I've been specially selected to..." Harry interjected with a mock guffaw. Jack scowled and continued, "... be in charge of this post to watch for the enemy coming up the valley." He pointed to the window. "And we are going to do it, acid-breath, understand? It could mean promotion, but what's it to you, eh?"

Harry turned away, sniggering.

By now the fourth private was awake and stood up, "Okay, Jack, sorry I mean corporal, it's my turn now. Give me the binoculars and you take a break."

Harry wouldn't let anything go. "Gawd blimey, Jim with the bino's, we're safe in our beds with a short-sighted git like you looking out of the window."

Andy had by now had enough, he leaned over the edge of the couch and grabbed Harry tightly by the collar, forcing his face close.

"Come on now, Harry. Stop bickering. I don't know what's got into you, but whatever it is go to the bog and get rid of it. This is a cushy number, dry and no action to speak of, and I for one am grateful for it. Enjoy it while you can."

He loosened his grip and roughly pushed Harry back onto the couch.

Harry thought for a moment, clearly outnumbered, and said begrudgingly, "The boys are right, *corporal*, we are at your service."

He stood up and gave a mock salute.

Jack's blood was up though; his authority had been challenged by this bad behaviour. It would take a few minutes to calm him.

"You make it sound as though you have a choice, soldier! As I said, it's a matter of honour and pride we do this and do it well."

He fumbled in his canvas bag for papers and a map.

Harry smirked. "Look, okay, I'm a bad lad, but I know that and everybody else does. Jim's right. Let's relax. I have a pack of cards and there's a few bottles of French plonk on that box over by the sink. One man can be on watch and the others take it easy. Duty will be done, and everyone's happy, eh?"

Jack didn't even look at him and said loudly, "No drinking on duty!"

Harry swore and threw the cards on the table like a sulky schoolboy.

"Oh, come on, corporal," said Andy calmly, "don't take any notice of him. We've been working hard getting this place set up and a bit of relaxation wouldn't go amiss."

"Don't try and tempt the General," Harry interjected.

"Shut it, Harry. That's your last warning." Jim pointed a finger at him and glared.

Jack was pleased with the tacit support from the other soldiers and confidently faced them all.

"That's enough. I'm in charge here. P'raps we could use a break. Maybe just a little wine while we play, but not much, understand? One man on watch at all times."

The mood instantly lightened, and Andy muttered his thanks. As he sat down, he noticed a small tube of ointment on the table with Harry's name on it, picked it up and read the label out loud.

"*PARASITOX, one shilling. Our boys pushing back the Hun have another formidable enemy, body vermin!* It says here, *prepared for you to resist attack, non-greasy and pleasant to use. Send it to your soldier friends.* Some friends you got, Harry!"

Harry snatched it back. "Yeah, friends. More than you, I bet. You can go on scratching your crotch and I'll carry on using this."

Andy laughed and imitated a monkey scratching his bits. He felt good, scoring a point against the belligerent Harry, and went to the sideboard, uncorked a bottle of wine, and poured some into glasses. Raising one to his nose he declared it fit for a king. "'Ere lads, we should have some with the ham that the neighbouring farmer gave us this morning."

Jim declared them to be *lucky boys* and toasted providence.

Jack looked on thoughtfully. "Yeah, we are lucky. My wife and kids don't have ham for their dinner. Things are tough. She works in a shell factory in Nottingham, the only industry that makes a profit out of all this. That's why we need to win this lot and get home, quickly."

"I'll drink to that," said Andy, seizing the moment. "Here's to victory."

Andy had always been the one to calm situations in barrack blocks or bars. It was his nature to smooth things over, but he was aware that he had his work cut out.

They all raised their glasses together. Jack only sipped, whilst the others quaffed. Harry leaned back on the couch, his arrogant posture every bit as sarcastic as his mouth.

Andy dealt the cards and Jim made an excuse to use the toilet. As he passed Jack, who was now standing by the door, he whispered, "Don't mind him, Jack. You're alright, y'know. I don't mind working for you. Just take it easy. We're all together in this place and have to get on. Take no notice of him."

He gave a backward glance to Harry who was ignoring the earlier exhortation not to imbibe too much.

Jack maintained watch by the window, looking earnestly through the binoculars. Jim returned, buttoning his fly, making a soldier's remark, "That's the missus's best friend seen to!" He sat down, sipped the wine, and picked up his cards. He was the easy-going joker of the squad and reasoned that so long as there was enough wine the mood would settle – besides, he was looking forward to this cushy number.

After a few hands of poker, Harry yawned and stretched. "Let's liven things up a bit – how about a shilling a hand?"

Jack looked around quickly, "No gambling, King's reg's."

Harry smirked but said nothing. Jim and Andy looked embarrassed and fidgeted.

Andy broke the silence and said persuasively, "What about a few pence a hand, corporal, can't do any harm eh?"

Although Jack hated gambling, he was in two minds because he felt he had to reward Andy and Jim for their loyalty. "Okay then. Special dispensation. Only pence and an overall limit of a shilling each person, per hand. Count me in too. Jim, you good for a watch duty?"

Jim jumped up, pulled his forelock, and clicked his heels. "Ja, Mein Kaiser," and everyone laughed, even Jack.

"I don't wanna play much anyway. I'm saving my money to buy one of those gramophone machines, His Master's Voice I think they are called. They cost five pounds and ten shillings. That's a lot of dosh. Then I'll set it up in my bedroom at home and entice a lass to come and listen to it. Ooh la la!"

"Yeah, but when they get to your room and see there are no bleedin' records, they'll know what you're up to!" said Andy.

This led to more ribald laughter and earned him a cushion across his head. He playfully pushed his comrade, "Let's spare your fantasies, Jim, you get back to the window watch for the Krauts and leave us grown-ups to play. "

He laughed and dealt the cards.

They played several hands, and each had a chance to win pennies, but none of the hands were that startling. After thirty minutes and more glasses of wine they began to enter the fool's paradise that is gambling.

Jack was banker again and dealt; Andy looked at his hand, "I'm in for two."

Harry declared he was in for one card and Jack went for three.

Andy opened with two pence and Jack raised him a penny. Harry smirked. "I'll raise you all for nine pence."

Andy glared him, "Not quite a shilling, but it is a bit steep this early on. What's your game Harry?"

Harry ignored the challenge. "You in or not?"

Andy grimaced, but agreed he was in.

Jack was staring at his cards and lost in the possibilities. "Okay, you little gob-shite, your nine pence and raise you three more."

"Ooh, corporal, so rude. Must mind your p's and q's, what with you being in charge and all that. You must set an example."

The baiting was blatant.

Jack felt uneasy. This was the classic example of being a leader but vulnerable through participation. He was experienced enough to know that games of chance rarely involve qualities of discipline and common sense. Lady Luck does not recognise rank. He cursed inwardly - why did he not follow Andy and drop out?

He decided to go no further and laid his cards down. "Three nines and a pair of jacks: full house I believe."

"Ah, dear old corporal, very good indeed. But not quite." Harry opened his hand with a flourish. "Four sixes, king high. Four of a kind beats a full house," and he triumphantly scooped the pot. "I should think you want to stop now, corporal, and I understand how painful it is to lose," he smirked.

"Not at all," said Jack, his blood up at the misfortune his full house had failed. "Deal now, get on with it."

Andy was painfully aware of the rising tension. He wished he could do something to help his corporal.

Harry smirked. "And of course, with your skills and bad luck you'll want to stay with pence and not shillings?"

"No," said Jack, his voice almost cracking "just one hand of shillings won't matter, why not?"

Andy blanched and Jim lowered his binoculars and looked over his shoulder in disbelief.

The cards were dealt, and Andy played as well as his hand would allow, but poker demands a commitment to bet, using your confidence and self-belief even with a poor hand, to force your opponent to quit. But with only a pair of tens he was unable to harness that much confidence and threw his hand in. That left Jack and Harry glaring at each other over the top of their cards.

Harry smiled and kept raising the stakes, a shilling at a time until the pot, now simply a piece of paper recording the bids, was over two pounds.

Eventually, when the pot reached over three pounds, Jack faltered and said, shakily, "I'll see you for one pound!"

Jim dropped the binoculars and turned towards the players – this was getting out of hand.

Harry then slowly lowered his cards. "Nice one General, now let's see what I have for you." First one king was laid on the table, then just a seven of diamonds, and Jack's heart beat hopefully. But his hopes were dashed as a triumphant Harry laid three more kings. Four of a kind again. Jack dropped his cards without revealing them.

"You win," he declared dejectedly.

"Oh, deary me, *corporal,* lucky old Harry. Well, this excitement has got the better of me, so I'll take a leak." He got up and sauntered through the door to the outside toilet.

Andy gave Jack a supportive look. "Look, don't take it to heart. Harry used to be a good bloke but got victimised by a sadistic RSM whose son got killed in an airship raid on London. He was permanently angry and took it out on everybody, but selected Harry for special treatment. He was an animal. He kept his platoon in an icy trench for six days and they all got trench foot. Harry's never taken to authority ever since. Chuck it in now, Jack."

"Corporal, you mean!"

"Okay, corporal. Just ease up will you. Jim and I are happy with you, we've said that. We're not baiting you, are we? As I say, chuck it in."

Jack's face was red, and Andy knew that he was not taking it in. Jack frowned and said unconvincingly, "Yeah, it's only a game. I tell the kids that. But I didn't mean to lose that much though."

"Kids? Got a picture?"

Jack quickly reached for his wallet and brought out a sepia photograph of a woman and two small boys and showed it to Andy. Jim came to the couch and looked over Andy's shoulder.

"What a lovely lady, Jack," said Jim. "You're a lucky feller, she's a beauty. I can see why you want to get home early. That's what we need Jack, something good to focus on, eh?"

Jack smiled weakly and nodded.

"Yeah. That's why I take my career seriously. I don't ever want to let her, or the army down."

The door creaked and Harry came back into the room, adjusting his dress as he did so. As he came back to the couch, he looked over Jack's shoulders.

"Very tasty. How come you get a woman like that, corporal?"

Andy glared at Harry. "Because he's a good guy, that's bloody why. Now sit down and shut up."

"Strewth, the team is very supportive. A good man, eh? He must be the only one with two tapes on his arm to be considered that way. I should be supportive too but just cannot bring myself to kiss the arses of authority. Never mind, for the moment we're playing poker. I think you need a chance to get some of your winnings back. What say. . . *corporal?*"

Jack was in a bad place. He had lost a lot of money and knew that he should stack – but the chance to get some cash back was tempting.

"Okay, I suppose so," he said resignedly.

The games that followed gradually brought Jack some of his cash back and he began to feel a little better.

However, there was still a considerable sum outstanding.

Harry though, had other ideas. "Oh well, it looks as though I'm on a losing streak. You've clawed back a pound and a few shillings, leaving you," he referred to the notebook, "exactly two pounds fifteen shillings owed to me. We'll make it interesting, we'll play one more hand. How About that? Five pounds to the winner. What say?"

Andy withdrew immediately, saying it was too much for him.

Jack's mind raced it could clear his debt and leave him with small change, but if he lost it would more than double his debt. His head ached with tension.

"But it needs bottle, *corporal,* bottle, not stripes!"

Andy stood up angrily. "I'm out, Jack," forgetting the title, "and so you should be."

Harry beamed. "Are they in charge or are you, *corporal?*"

Jack blanched and glared at Harry. "Do it. And keep your trap shut throughout!" he barked.

It seemed like an age as the cards were dealt, they made a clicking sound as they hit the wooden table. Each man scooped them up and without a word exchanged two each. They sat staring at their hands. Finally, Harry spoke. "Well, as I said, no betting. Just a straight lay. Will you go first, or shall I?"

Jack swallowed nervously. He indicated he was to lay his cards down first. He had two pairs, jacks and nines, ace singleton. Harry just sat still.

"Go on then," said Jack, "get it over with."

63

Harry triumphantly threw his cards on the table, revealing two pairs, queens, and tens. Jack's face went white. What had he done?

Harry didn't stop. "We can always cut the cards for another five quid, what say?"

"No, enough's enough."

"Oh dear, why am I not surprised."

"What do you mean by that?" said Jack furiously.

"It's clear. You're dishonourable, that's what. I bet you're broke!"

"You watch your mouth, infantryman."

"Oh, sorry. I forgot. You're a good man with two tapes and a lovely family. But I have to say that a family man doesn't gamble away hard cash that can feed his kids. Poker and French tarts perhaps. So, I don't expect to see any cash from you, *corporal!*"

Jack lurched across the table and narrowly missed Harry's collar. He lost all sense of discipline. If he had caught him, he would have beaten him.

Harry jumped off the couch, and Andy quickly restrained Jack.

"Bastard!" Jack shouted.

Harry persisted. "So, where's the cash then?"

Andy squared up to Harry. "You're an odious cretin, Harry. I swear I'll swing for you one day."

Jack was demolished. He had misguidedly lost control and had to be supported by the other two infantrymen. He must pay up and regain his position – he had no choice. But he had no cash on him.

"I'll pay."

"How," sneered Harry, "bottle tops?"

Jack wrestled free from Andy and made for the door.

"Where are you going?" said Jim.

"Back to the lines. I have cash in my locker at the base in Beaurair. I'll be gone less than an hour. Keep watch,

Jim, you're in charge. This is my stupid fault, I dropped my guard and I'm gonna put it right."

At the door, he turned towards Harry and pointed at him.

"When I get back, you'll get your money and I'm gonna sort you out, I promise you that!"

Then he was gone, the sound of his rickety bicycle working its way across the gravel was all that could be heard.

Andy kicked over the table and it fell against Harry who remained expressionless. Jim resumed his position at the window.

Harry tried to get back in with his comrades. "Let him go, lads. Look, this is a cushy number and if we don't control that career minded gunner, he'll have us doing bayonet practice before breakfast, eh?"

He gave a half-laugh but failed to gain the attention of the others.

Jim angrily went back to the window to avoid talking to Harry.

He scanned the starlit horizon with his binoculars. Suddenly his face contorted in horror. "My God!"

Harry laughed. "Ah, the General is on his way back then, too far for his little legs?"

Jim's lips trembled, "No, we should've been looking, it's..."

The lights in the room dimmed and there was the sound of rifle-fire, shellfire, and blinding flashes pierced the windows. The room swirled as if in a vortex. As it did so, Marie Lloyd's voice and all manner of music hall songs of WWI filled the air. Eventually, it faded and there was stillness, until a jagged radio hiss crackled in the background. Then it cleared and a cultured deep male voice read a military bulletin.

This is General Routine Order Number 18850 and is given for the information of all military personnel in *France. Number 12703 Corporal J Apsley, Royal Artillery, was tried by Field Court Martial on the following charge:*

Misbehaving before the enemy, in such as a way as to show cowardice.

The accused was seen cycling away from the forward observation position 436 in the face of the advancing enemy, leaving his colleagues without supervision and failing to alert the main HQ that subsequently suffered many casualties.

The sentence of the court was that he should suffer death by firing squad. The sentence was carried out at 7 a.m. on 30 May 1917.

The apparition of the WWI corporal rushed out of the farmhouse, fell to his knees, and put his hands to his head, screaming, but no words came out.

10

Verisimilitude

Gordon straightened his tie and inspected his attire in the mirror. He combed a full head of silver hair and clipped his moustache. Satisfied with his appearance, he left his small flat in Horsham and drove to Gatwick airport, where he parked in the short stay car park and made his way to the South Terminal. Under his arm he carried a sign that read: Mr Ahmed Sadique.

Once inside the arrivals area he joined several other men all carrying cards with names on; some were European, and others were quite unpronounceable. There was time for a quick cup of coffee and a croissant – the others preferred bacon sandwiches. They greeted him like old friends and jokes were exchanged about the state of politics in the UK, football, and the increasing traffic problems in the local area.

A younger member of the group teased him. "You still voting Conservative Gordon? With a car like yours you look as though you are friends with Rupert Murdoch."

Gordon smiled broadly. Because of his smartness and his 'fancy car' as they called it, the others deferred to him; he was realistic and suspected it was more of an age thing.

He responded in a jovial and confident manner. "I'll ignore that young man, when you've seen proper life beyond your red-top newspaper you can tease me all you like."

The others laughed and the young man playfully bowed.

Gordon always took an interest in their family situations and asked pertinent questions, remembering every detail. He enjoyed the camaraderie, it gave him a buzz, contact and a reason for being.

No one ever asked specific questions about each other's customers. The other drivers had seen Gordon's old marque Jaguar saloon, which was in pristine condition, with highly polished black paintwork and old-fashioned chrome. They envied him. Most of them purchased cars from auctions, which were spacious and gave customers a bit of luxury but were not at all exciting.

"Okay, lads. Gates are open," said an Asian driver called Asif.

It was time to move to the arrivals gate, cards in hand, some written perfectly legibly and others rather less so. One by one the drivers collected their customers and waved to Gordon as they left – a strange ritual of belonging, deferring to an older man of stature; he politely acknowledged each one in turn.

When a flight from the Middle East arrived, Gordon feigned anxiety and surveyed the passengers as they passed through the gate and into the airport reception area. He quickly moved forward, bidding the remaining drivers farewell with a smile and a wave, and walked steadily towards to a man of middle eastern appearance, who was dressed in a beige suit and carried a leather overnight bag.

"Excuse me, sir, I do hate to bother you," he said, as he briskly walked alongside the man. "But do you happen to know a Mr Sadique? I was sure he was on this flight – I do hope that I haven't missed him?"

They continued walking and as the man spoke to him, Gordon glanced at his fellow drivers who enviously watched him go with what looked like a well-healed customer, before returning their attention to the passengers exiting the arrivals gate.

The man smiled and said he did not know any Mr Sadique. Gordon politely kept the conversation going announcing that he must have missed his customer and apologising for interrupting the man. The man smiled and turned down the offer of a lift, which Gordon expected, saying he had his own car. They both walked on in the same direction.

"I need to collect another customer anyway, so I may treat myself to a coffee or two." Gordon chatted amiably about the weather and as they crossed the road immediately in front of the South Terminal one of the other drivers drove past with his charge in the back and waved at Gordon, who returned the gesture.

The drive home to Horsham was short and Gordon got out of the Jaguar, inspecting its bodywork as he did so; he resolved to give it another polish, despite having cleaned it only yesterday. In his flat he collected his mail, consisting almost entirely of bills and advertisements, and made himself a cup of coffee.

As he rubbed the name from the card he thought carefully. What name for tomorrow, he wondered? Should he choose something unusual or rather ordinary, Johnson or De Vere perhaps? Yes, De Vere would be much better, because it was easy to get into conversation with strangers if the name was unusual or rather superior in its format. He wrote it neatly on the card, putting it carefully on the hall table ready for his next trip to the airport, then made a mental note that one of the drivers had a daughter who was in hospital and would ask after her tomorrow. He would also congratulate another on becoming a grandfather for the first time.

Gordon settled in a comfortable chair in the lounge for a short break, opened the Times newspaper and turned to the crossword, which he would allow himself one hour to complete.

As he sipped his coffee he glanced at the photograph of his late wife, Doris, and smiled his usual morning greeting, as he had done for the last six years since she died.

11

The Edge

Why the hell not? His life was so complicated; beautiful in parts and yet wounded by the pinpricks of emotional darts that dug deep. A red mist enveloped Pete's mind causing him so much pain he wanted to retch. It just wouldn't go away; or was it that he wouldn't let it?

Through rheumy eyes he could just make out the swirling waters of the river Thames below, inky black in the night sky, with sparkling patches of light reflected from the nearby buildings and lamp posts lining its edge. The steel beam below his feet felt icy cold, alien to his touch. He wondered how long he had stood there. He moved his foot a little and nearly lost his balance; a shock surged through his body.

He reflected on how stupid that was. Why the fear when he was intent on falling anyway? This act was deemed to be the most selfish of all, yet it was the unconscious selfishness of those around him that brought him to it. Everyone considered him to be strong and focused, able to take the exigencies of life on the chin. How wrong they were.

His mind was in turmoil, and he fought hard to try and reason with the irrational voice in his head that urged him to give up.

As he struggled with dark thoughts, he heard a sound of breathing. He slid his feet quietly back along the beam, careful of the protruding rivets and saw the unmistakable trace of breath vapour in the chilly night air. There in the dimness, was a woman holding tight to a steel beam.

Courage almost failed him, but he stuttered, "Hello...."

The woman gasped and said angrily, "What the....! Go away, for God's sake, leave me alone."

"Who are you?" he said quietly.

"I said go away, don't you listen? Don't come any closer, I will jump, and I mean it, now just sod off."

As she moved, her foot skidded off the side of a large rivet, and she wrapped her arms around the upright beam, and let out a yelp as she grasped it tightly to her. Jack's heart nearly stopped.

"Careful, please. I'm not going to interfere, I promise."

The woman was silent for then said falteringly, "I bloody mean it, you know, I really do."

His heart was beating fast, and he breathed hard, and his mind worked overtime.

"Oh dear, that's a bit tricky. You see, being a gentleman, I would be forced to go in after you," impulsively adding, "I'm sure your problems can be solved."

He frowned at the stupidity of this prosaic peace of wisdom, given his own circumstances.

The woman sniffed back tears. He could just make out her features and blonde hair.

"Maybe so, but either way, lovely man, I'm doomed, so let's just face the inevitable, eh?"

Pete was shocked. "Wanna talk?"

"No."

"Why not?"

"You're a persistent sod, mister lovely man. What's it to you?"

"Well, I, er, that's to say, I feel the same way."

The woman's gaze pierced the gloom. Was she summing him up? Or was it just his imagination – after all, it was his imagination that caused all his misery?

The woman let out a sudden gasp.

"Good grief, you and I are here to do the same bloody thing."

She laughed loudly.

"Tell you what, I'll have that bit of river over there and you can have that bit below, looks a bit muddy to me."

He smiled and although weak it was probably for the first time in months. Strangely the pain in his head lessened, it was as though he had already fallen into the cold river water and the shock had recharged his brain.

"Hmmm, not sure that's at all fair. Could we draw straws?"

"Listen, mister lovely man, I told you, I daren't move a finger, let alone draw a bloody straw!"

Despite her fear she tried to move, slowly and cautiously.

"Please take care," he blurted. "I shouldn't joke, sorry."

After a short silence, she spoke softly. "Do *you* want to talk?"

Pete breathed heavily, paused, and said unsteadily, "I'm really not sure."

Her voice was now softer and less agitated. "Easy now. Look, I will, if you will. We both have nothing to lose."

Pete plucked up courage to discuss what he had always considered out of bounds.

"Okay, here goes. I'm a widower. I fell in love and never fell out; we were married for thirty years. My wife was killed in a car accident. No one's fault. Just tragic, that's all. I grieve, for sure, often, but resolved not to let it take over my whole being. I've been trying to make a new life with a lady, but, well, my mind will just not let go of things: the challenge of new love and guilt letting down the memory of my wife, my independence, a fear of being controlled, suspicion. Goodness me, the list is enormous. Most hurtful was my son's resentment of my new partner. The way he looked at me sent arrows through my heart to my wife in heaven. My friends are sweet, but they just want to keep Alice's memory alive and seal me in aspic. Oh, heck, have you ever heard such crap. Sorry."

The sound of a Thames boat carrying partygoers along the river broke the silence. There is surely nothing more irritating to the depressed than the sound of people being jolly and happy; the contrast made the sad situation even more painful.

The woman peered down at the river. "Glad we didn't go just then, we might have landed on the quartet or the chicken curry!"

It was disarming, she was having a strange effect on him.

"Okay, now it's your turn," he said, "fair's fair."

Pete heard her take a deep breath.

"I've got breast cancer. My mum and best friend had it and it killed them. I've also had to come to terms with facts about myself. I'm a control freak, well, not such a freak really, but just someone who likes to control. I never really noticed it until I was forced to confront it after my divorce and some unfortunate work situations. I just like things right, know what I mean? I'm not a bad person, I think I

74

am quite fun really. Now this. The doctors mean well, but I can see through their expressions and wish-washy words. Have this operation, do this chemotherapy, take these pills, yeah, yeah...I've heard it all before. And, sorry, I don't know your name?"

"Pete."

"Ah, mine's Hannah. Well, Pete, the thought of ending up feeble in a hospital bed saying goodbye to the world, with people dribbling into their hankies fills me with dread."

"That's a bit harsh. When was your diagnosis?"

"What the hell does that matter?" Hannah huffed irritably.

"It matters because much of what you just said – sorry but I tend to tell it how it is – is based on fantasy. On what you don't want to happen rather than what is most likely to happen. Hannah, many women have surgery and chemo and survive, more than those that die. If your diagnosis is recent there's a chance. Besides, listening to you I'm convinced that with your spirit you would, for sure, control your way to survival."

A noisy speedboat passed below them and seemed to underscore his rationale.

"Pete, thank you. You're quite a caring guy, you know that?" She paused and added resignedly, "So, it seems that I have an illogical mind surrounded by emotional barbed wire. Well then, what about you? You're not surely just trying to pinch my place in the water?"

"No, it's yours, be my guest, take it. I can always earmark somewhere else."

The emerging exchange of dark humour and all the words began to melt their purpose.

He added, carefully, "My new partner was like you. You have a calm cheerful voice, Hannah, so did she. I drove her away because I failed to confront all my worries and, frankly, I was a pain in the arse. Good grief, this is so crazy, here I am ready to end my life and I meet you. It's so strange, I find myself wanting to save you. To reach out and hold you tight. To protect you and say everything is going to be all right."

Hannah clung tightly to the beam and touched her forehead against it.

"Hell, my dear Pete, that's just how I feel. Your story is so touching. I want to encourage you to meditate or relax, or...well, any bloody thing that will let you see yourself and your situation clearly. Sorry, I know that's the controller in me. Isn't it ironic, we care more about others than we do ourselves?"

They stared at each other's blurry images through the blackness.

"Hannah, I'm not sure about you, but the fizz seems to have gone out of my bid for oblivion." He had by now moved close enough to reach out and touch her hand. It felt soft and warm despite the chilly air. "Let's leave this place."

Hannah's hand turned and closed over his. "I guess so."

They cautiously made their way along the edge of the bridge to the gap in a wire fence that allowed them illegal access. Pete helped her through it and onto a metal walkway leading to steps down to the pavement. The streetlights appeared blindingly bright, and they had to stand for a while and let their eyes adjust.

Strangely, it was like another world.

Pete stamped his feet noisily on the damp pavement and turned his collar up. "I feel so bloody stupid."

"Yeah, so do I," Hannah put her hands to her face. "I could cry, in fact I think I will."

"I feel like that too but won't. *Man-thing*, you know!"

Hannah looked up and tried to smile through the tears that trickled down her cheeks. "I just think I need to go home for a *coffee-thing.*"

Bright lights lit up the street and a taxi came towards them. Pete stepped into the road and waved it down. Hannah got in and wound down the window. "Take care lovely man."

Pete said nothing but gave her a playful salute as the taxi drove off. When it was fifty yards away, he suddenly put his hands to his head and cursed.

Was he too old? Was he a coward?

He sprinted down a steep grassy embankment and almost fell into the road at the bottom just as the taxi turned a corner and came towards him. He waved it down.

"You're making a habit of this," said the driver.

Pete ignored him and opened the door. Hannah looked surprised.

"Look, sorry. I, er, well I wondered. When is your next consultant's appointment?"

"What?"

"Well, I'd really like to be there to support you. I don't need to come in, really, I'd be happy to sit outside. Afterwards we could, er, go for a *coffee-thing* perhaps?"

Hannah sat back in her seat, smiled, and thought, "Why not, indeed. Why not."

12

Seeds From Mars

James held his lover's hand tightly as they gambolled through the thick grass, looking at the unusual bright coloured lights that appeared fleetingly in the night sky – he had never felt happier. Here was a woman who loved him despite his hearing loss, and who made every effort to learn sign language. It was late autumn and the full moon shone as bright as a torch on them both as they ran towards a large pond; Rosalyn signalled that she wanted to dip her toes in the water, kissed him lightly, wrestled her hand free and ran ahead.

As they drew near the pond, James saw the shimmering water through gaps in large clumps of reeds and small trees; a faint mist obscured it at first, but it became clearer the closer they came. Moonlight sparkled on the surface. On they ran, and Rosalyn drew slightly ahead of him. She had always been fitter and tonight she was particularly lively, laughing and waving, crazy in her happiness.

Suddenly, she half fell to the ground, then looked up at him with an anguished, frightened gaze, her mouth wide open as if screaming – unheard by James. She appeared to be holding her ears as if blocking out extreme noise. Every time she tried to get up to move back towards him, she fell down again, and frighteningly appeared to be dragged towards the pond. James was horrified and unable to help her. - panic filled his body. He saw her raised arms thrashing as they moved through the reeds then disappearing.

James shouted but was aware of his verbal limitations. He was scared and then tearful with rage, unable to help. Where did Rosalyn go? What was happening?

Almost imperceptibly, he felt his ears throbbing, very slightly, and to his horror, the roots of the reeds that he was standing on began to move around his feet. He jumped with fear, turned, and ran, tripping slightly as if something had reached for his ankles.

His eyes were glazed, and he could hardly see, and his chest heaved with emotional gasps of air. He was so upset he was unaware of where he was and stumbled from one piece of land to another, through trees and fields and, unbeknown to him, around in ever widening circles. He just wanted help.

After fifteen minutes he fell to the ground, exhausted and helpless. His eyes filled with tears of frustration, when he was startled by bright round lights suddenly surrounding him, then two more large ones glaring down on him from the air.

He passed out cold.

On waking, one hour later, James stumbled through the grass and eventually reached a road, along which he staggered for about two miles. As he fell to his knees, a car approached. It stopped and a woman got out, saying kindly, "Are you all right, dear?"

Curtis Redpath ran his fingers through his rain-damp fair hair. He stood alongside other local journalists outside the Royal Bournemouth Hospital, notebook in one hand, hot coffee in a plastic mug in the other. Hunching his large shoulders, he turned to another journalist on his left who rather disturbingly looked like his irascible newspaper editor.

"What's all this about then?"

"Well, now, young Curtis, that's the big question. It seems that lad of the name of, let's see," he referred to his notebook, "ah yes, here it is, James Dunn, was walking out with his girlfriend, in the local fields late last night." He gave a conspiratorial wink and continued. "He claims she was 'taken', by something sinister."

Curtis huffed and sipped the coffee, finding it difficult to concentrate through his monumental hangover after a late night of poker and a surfeit of single malt whisky with friends. He resented his rehabilitation to sobriety being interrupted by what appeared to be no more than a "missing person" story.

Journalism offered high hopes of campaigning and researching for the common good, unveiling bad deeds or corporate deception. Instead, he found himself confined to a local newspaper reporting charitable deeds, vandalism, and the general self-aggrandisement of local politicians, keen to display their good side – or at least whatever they could conjure up.

He recalled the most amusing report he ever covered, which was when a local farmer dumped a truckload of manure outside the local authority headquarters because his planning permission for a barn had been turned down. That was two years ago. Since then, the job had been utterly boring and he filled his out of work hours by joining the Territorial Army and doing charity work; it was commendable, but unexciting. He felt unchallenged and unfulfilled, but he knew in his heart that he had not really applied himself as well as he should have done. He was pretty fed up.

"What else do we know?" he said, feigning interest.

"Not much," said the other reporter, "except that he's profoundly deaf. It makes the interviewing a bit difficult I suppose, so they sent for an interpreter. I think they are having difficulty finding one."

Curtis thought for a moment and his energy quickly returned. He learned British Sign Language level two only last year so that he could work as a volunteer for a local charity that supported deaf people. Here was an opportunity to get an interview and steal a march on his contemporaries.

He made an excuse to visit the toilet and walked straight towards the hospital entrance. Journalism can be a dirty business, but he was beyond scruples and thought only of the possibility of getting an interview, a story line, then getting back to his bed-sit for a nightcap and an early rendezvous with his duvet. He strode confidently into the hospital entrance and approached reception, glad that today of all days he had managed to dress smartly in a sports jacket, blue denim shirt and chinos.

He held his overcoat across his arm.

A stern-faced receptionist, with grey hair in a bun and reading spectacles hanging on a cord over her paisley blouse, regarded him imperiously.

"Can I help you?"

"Yes. I'm here to communicate with the poor chap, James Dunn I believe his name is, who was found wandering in the countryside last night. He's deaf and I believe you want an interpreter?"

Her expression brightened straight away.

"Why, yes, he's on the second floor, ward six, a private room." She frowned benevolently, "and be gentle with him,

I think he's been through a terrible experience. Some people think it's an odd story, but I think they're being pretty cruel."

Curtis thanked her profusely and made his way to ward six.

Outside the ward sat a policewoman absorbed with her mobile phone and obviously quite bored. It didn't take long to gain access to the room, based on the fact that this was not considered a criminal case, rather, the police did not want the young man to stray before they had a chance to interview him about his missing girlfriend.

Curtis went into the ward without knocking. It had only one small bedside cabinet, one chair for a visitor and an overhead gantry of some kind that had various instruments on it squeezed into a corner. A slightly built young man, with long dark hair and a pale youthful complexion sat on the bed with his head in his hands. His face was red, and his eyes appeared swollen.

The young man opened his eyes wide and frowned when he saw Curtis, then looked alarmed and stood up.

Curtis quickly gave a big smile and a thumbs-up and signed to him, "It's okay, you can trust me." This calmed the young man slightly and he looked less anxious.

Aware that the boy had reportedly lost his lover, Curtis felt wretched; was a story worth it? He signed, "What happened?"

Over the next fifteen minutes, amid waving arms and frightened expressions, the story unfolded. Curtis asked whether he remembered where he had been, but the young man was too distressed and confused. Had he talked to anyone else? No, only to a local policeman, who had asked him to draw some images.

He showed them to Curtis.

The sketches were of stick-like forms for simplicity. One depicted his girlfriend seemingly tangled in what appeared to be plant-like shapes, being dragged towards a shimmering mist. She was holding her hands to her head and the sketch resembled the Edvard Munch's modernist painting *The Scream*. It was frightening to look at; even more so to consider that this was a contemporary account of something that had really happened, not a science-fiction horror story.

The second sketch showed just her arm amidst a tangle of plants, with the mist again patchy around about. The third and final sketch was of bright lights in a semi-circle and two even brighter large ones above them, with the man on his knees as they closed in.

Curtis now regarded James with genuine sympathy and gone was the objective of quick soundbites for the sake of a cheap headline.

He could not lie to him. Cautiously, he explained that he was a journalist and wanted to help. The man became distressed and started to look aggressive at this news. Curtis raised both palms facing outwards, then brought his right hand to his heart, mouthing,

"It is okay. I promise."

Using what little skills he had, he signed to James that he would visit him again, perhaps at his home, repeating that he was not to worry and that he genuinely wanted to help. The man was mollified and scribbled down his address and mobile telephone number.

Curtis left the ward quietly and spied a smartly dressed woman accompanied by a policeman approaching from the end of the corridor. Sensing that this was the bone fide interpreter, he turned about and used a different set of stairs to get back to the entrance.

It was a chilly walk back to his flat. When he was inside and settled, he sat down to write a brief account of the incident and his first-hand discussions with James Dunn. He still had to earn his bread but wanted to write something more than just a sensational headline garnered from a variety of quotes. When he finished, he promised readers that more was to follow as the police investigation continued, and then emailed it to his editor. After making a strong cup of coffee and regretting his three A.M. return home the previous night, he fell onto the bed and quickly drifted off to sleep.

There are television presenters one likes, and others that set teeth on edge, so much so that seeing them encourages a quick tap of the remote to access the next channel. Curtis awoke to the sound of the local late evening news, as the television activated via the time switch; he reached for the remote control. The urbane presenter was doing his best to look earnest and self-important as he described in lengthy and sombre tones what was clearly an interesting case, relieving his boring newscasting life of dog shows, road closures and local charity events. The screen showed an ambulance leaving with James Dunn en route to the local police station.

Curtis sat bolt upright as the sketches that James had drawn were put on the screen; he was transfixed. The presenter then turned to Curtis's least favourite character, Miles Pinkerton, a grey-haired, bespectacled man who regarded himself as a bit of a polymath, and an expert on everything from lug worms to astronomy.

Pinkerton was also an absolute pain on the subject of Unidentified Flying Objects, writing countless letters to the local papers offering to do a column or article. Curtis could not believe that this charlatan had been able to get in front of the camera.

He was introduced, then dramatically took off his spectacles and stared at the camera. "Many of you know that I am somewhat an expert on the subject of UFOs. Let me be clear that these sketches show the abduction of a young woman by visitors from outer space. This last sketch, made by the young man who was with her at the time, is an accurate depiction of a flying saucer. There is no doubt whatever about that."

He paused and cleaned his spectacles.

"I am also of no doubt that the incident took place at Dundry Hill, just above the reservoir, about three miles from where young James Dunn was found. This hill has been of interest to me for some years it has what I regard as marks made by a large space craft. The soil also has high radiation readings. I will be preparing more information on this over the coming weeks."

Curtis groaned. How had the sketches got to Pinkerton and the television company? The local policeman, a nurse or cleaner perhaps? Bastards! It was all academic really. They had been leaked and now the story would grow itself.

James Dunn sat in a wicker chair in his ground floor flat in Christchurch, his face in his hands and eyes tight shut. What had happened? Where was his lovely Rosalyn? Was she okay? His breakfast lay on the table untouched. Did the police take him seriously? It was so difficult to communicate everything, but he knew what he saw – he was not hallucinating!

All his life he had had to fight for whatever he wanted. His deafness meant that he had to learn a whole new language – indeed, BSL was just that, another language, like German or French. But the journey through education to independence had been fraught, what with teasing from his childhood classmates, through the process of learning from specialist tutors, and on to university.

Like so many deaf people, he endured it all stoically and made a success of education, eventually earning a 2:1 degree from Sussex University. Dating had been difficult too. Who wants to date a chap who, though handsome, talks with a kind of low slur, because he cannot hear his own voice?

Darling Rosalyn didn't mind. She loved him and he cherished her. Now she was gone, God knows where.

He shouted at the policeman who interviewed him in the hospital, the fool kept on asking stupid questions and thought that talking very loudly would do the trick - as if that would bridge total deafness! The patronising expression on the policeman's face made him mad as hell and it was made worse when he laughed at his sketches. James stood up threateningly, as if to punch him. That quietened him down.

Although slightly built, he was swarthy and his dark eyes telegraphed menace when he wanted them to. James knew how to look after himself and didn't take prisoners. It was difficult trying to work out what happened and was all so confusing. No one wanted to connect with him, everyone jumped to conclusions of their own and the situation was treated like a piece of entertainment, rather than a crime scene. That would not find Rosalyn. The local brainbox, Miles Pinkerton was no better.

James had seen lights for sure but did not believe for a moment that it was a UFO. Nor did he believe that he and Rosalyn had been anywhere near Dundry Hill, another stupid conclusion. He felt so angry because no one would listen.

A light signal flashed on the apartment wall, meaning someone was at the door. He opened it and saw Cutis who had a bottle of single malt in his hand with a tilt of his head and a half smile. James was relieved and let him in.

This man would listen to him.

Curtis made a sign for glasses and sat down on a settee opposite the wicker chair. James brought two from the sideboard and opened the bottle and poured the whisky. He offered Curtis a cigarette, which was accepted gratefully – not many people smoke these days.

Curtis faced James directly and used every ounce of his BSL revision that morning, to communicate. The discussion took a while, to James's occasional amusement, as he stumbled through signing, and slowly but surely a picture emerged. He brought out a map of the local area and James became convinced that he and Rosalyn had been nowhere near Dundry Hill at all. Curtis had also spent an hour that morning, making calls to transport agencies, and eventually talked to a bus driver on the route, Christchurch to Bournemouth, who remembered dropping the couple along Matcham's Lane. He was so certain he marked this point in pencil on the map.

They both stared silently at the contours and shapes, on the chart; James grew animated and pointed to an oval shape, making waving movements with his hand indicating water.

"What is it, what can you see?"

He looked at the map and signed, "A pond of some sort, is that it?"

At this remark, James's breathing became laboured, and he signed the story of Rosalyn grasping her head.

Curtis looked at him directly, pointing to the sides of his head as he signed.

"Her ears perhaps, she was suffering from some kind of loud noise?"

James held his hands out palms upwards and mouth tilted down at both sides. He did not know for sure what was going on.

Curtis thought hard about the facts: water, large plants wrapped around Rosalyn and her apparent agony at some kind of noise. He idly moved his finger around the circle and stopped abruptly. Nearby, there was an airport runway: Bournemouth International airport; and airports have lights.

The television on the wall, which had been on silent with sub-titles automatically switched on to audio and there was the pompous Miles Pinkerton standing in front of a television crew on a misty Dundry Hill, surrounded by gazebos of different kinds and people prodding the ground with walking sticks. He wondered what they hoped to find. Pinkerton was discussing UFOs and his theory about the abduction of Rosalyn. A small crowd of people was earnestly asking questions, some of which were plain bonkers. Curtis blanched at the sight of it all. He knew that the man was completely wrong and resignedly referred back to the map, as much a means of escape from the television than to find clues.

"James, we have no choice, we are going to have to drive to this area," he signed, "can you do this?"

James took a deep breath and gave a half-enthusiastic thumbs-up sign, and they got their coats.

The drive from Christchurch to Matcham's Lane was short and James was very wound up and fidgeted constantly. Soon they were climbing over a metal gate and stumbling through undergrowth along a ragged cart track. James's steps faltered and Curtis had to encourage him to continue. They walked on cautiously, James looking left and right nervously. All of a sudden Curtis felt his head throbbing and heard a piercing whine; it was painful and got progressively louder. He was forced to put his hands over his ears, but it did not prevent the noise.

Touching James's arm, to reassure him, he noticed that he was frozen to the spot, looking at a large pond, shrouded by the late evening mist. He seemed unaffected by any sound and just stared open-mouthed at it. Curtis was beginning to lose focus and felt dizzy. He had to draw on inner strength to grab James's arm and force him to get back down the track to the gate. The pain in his ears was excruciating, but he kept stumbling in the opposite direction to the pond. Eventually back at their vehicle he fell to his knees and retched violently. Afterwards he stood up, panting, before eventually gaining his breath. James, unaffected by the sound, looked quizzically at him.

Curtis waited a while before driving back to the flat. Once inside, it took a while to compose himself.

James made coffee and they sat facing each other, so that Curtis could see his lips and face.

"James," he signed, looking stern and angry, "could you hear or feel any sound at all? I could and it was terrible." He paused and continued carefully. "From what you tell me Rosalyn was clearly holding her ears and seemed in agony."

James confirmed he did feel a slight tingling in his ears, but no more, then he broke down and Curtis moved away to give him space. It had been a traumatic experience. However, there was no doubt in Curtis's mind that he had found the site of Rosalyn's disappearance and that there was something very odd and frightening about it. If he was to solve this mystery, he had to engage with all the facts – and fast.

The local television news reacted excitedly to James's story, fuelled by the outpourings from Miles Pinkerton. It was not just these elements that drove the story, rather, the reports coming in about people whose relatives had gone missing and presumed to have run away, lost animals and even a horse and rider. Miles Pinkerton was in his element and stitched all manner of his own suppositions to these facts to support his UFO theories. The story just ran itself.

Curtis thought long and hard. There was nothing for it; he and James would have to go back to the pond, off Matcham's Lane, and look for evidence. He recalled deafness training and remembered that profoundly deaf people could experience some vibrations but were unlikely to hear anything unless they were fitted with a cochlear implant. James readily conceded that the loud sound did not affect him, therefore he was best placed to get close to the pond. He needed no persuasion. He would take a camera with a long-range lens and would turn and run if he experienced anything untoward.

Curtis explained to James that this was the only way they could secure evidence concerning Rosalyn's disappearance.

The next day, at dusk, they made their way again to Matcham's Lane. Luckily, James was competent with a camera and motivated to solve the disappearance of his lover.

"James," Curtis signed, holding his gaze intently, "remember what I said, only go as far as you feel safe. Take as many photographs as you can, then come back to me quickly. No heroics. Do you understand?"

James gave a wan smile and nodded.

Curtis drove as fast as he could along the country roads as the sun began to set. As he reached the location, he had to overtake a stationary fuel tanker that had its hazard lights on and engine running. The rear offside tyre displayed a wide split down the middle the driver had walked on a about thirty metres or so in order to get a better mobile signal and was talking animatedly into his mobile phone. He parked the car near a double gate and the track that led to the pond.

They got out of the car and without further briefing James began tentatively walking along path. Curtis followed but resolved that any sign of a high-pitched sound and he would turn and head back to the road as quickly as possible.

James moved along the track for about a mile, and as expected, felt a slight tingle in his skull. When the pond came into view, he repeatedly took pictures, to get used to the camera controls. He quickened his pace to the pond with the camera raised, panning the lens around the site, and took pictures at random. As he was about to lower the camera, he noticed the unmistakable shape of a horse's saddle, half submerged in the slimy shallows. Further on, to his horror, he saw shapes of a walking stick, a pair of boots and what looked like a backpack. Then the mist thickened. As he turned to run, he realised that something was trying to wrap itself around his left ankle and yelled with fright; it was the shape of bindweed, but thicker, and moved like a snake.

James furiously kicked out at the binding plant, but it curled around his ankle and held fast. He knew he had to act quickly and reached into his jacket pocket where he kept a cigarette lighter. He brought out the gas lighter and clicked it to produce a flame, then held it against the plant. To his relief the plant appeared to recoil and weakened its grip, and he wasted no time in disentangling his ankle and running up the incline of the track as fast as he could.

Curtis saw James running towards him waving the camera, his face full of fear. Curtis looked at the digital photographs and his eyes widened. He considered the evidence: reports of missing persons and animals, James's description of the incident and now these pictures; something very evil was in or around the pond area. Suddenly, a loud sound filled the air and he looked to the left and saw in the now darkening sky the shape of an approaching airliner coming into the airport. It had two large lights on the front of the fuselage and as it approached the runway, a line of bright approach lights went on. So, there was no UFO after all, just returning tourists from the continent in a big jet.

They hurried back to the car. James tended his sore ankle with cream from the first aid kit. Curtis felt agitated and his mind was racing. Up ahead, walkers with torches dallied as they chose paths to walk on and children chased a dog between hunks of grass. How could he stop them? Who would believe him? He was not even sure he could believe it himself. More to the point, would anyone else perish if he took no action? The situation weighed heavily on him, and he put his head in his hands. *Think, man, think!* He knew that there was no time to waste – something had to be done, now.

When he looked up, he noticed the fuel tanker in the rear-view car mirror. He knew exactly what he had to do. Leaving the confused James to tend his sores, he raced to the tanker. Luckily, the driver was a long way from the vehicle, still shouting and gesticulating into his mobile telephone. Curtis gingerly climbed into the driver's cab and felt the rumble of the engine ticking over; the keys were still in the ignition.

He gingerly put the vehicle into gear and tried not to make a noise, but the components clunked loudly. The driver heard the noise, dropped his mobile phone, and waved frantically, but there was no stopping now. The tanker kangarooed through the gears and reached about ten miles an hour, not fast, but this was like a rhinoceros on wheels. It was easy to overtake their own parked vehicle, but Curtis knew that smashing through the metal gate would need more traction and put his foot firmly on the accelerator, which responded with a growl.

James looked up surprised and saw Curtis at the wheel of the fuel tanker as it passed the car and gasped as it turned immediately left.

The tanker careered successfully through the gate, smashing it open, snapping the locked chain like plasticine. Curtis kept control. The noise of the flat-tyred rear wheel scraping on the ground was loud and shrill, and sparks flew about. As expected, the closer he went, the more painful became the high-pitched sound in his head. He steeled himself and drove on to the top of the incline that led down to the pond. The noise was simply too much for him and he had to stop. Dizzy but with a powerful sense of purpose, he staggered along the side of the tanker opening all the fuel outlets but cursed when the petrol failed to spill out.

He then remembered from his days in the Territorial Army, that air had to get in at the top to allow the fuel to discharge, so he scrambled on top of the vehicle and located three screw top openings held only by split pins that were thankfully, unlocked. He removed the pins and wrenched the tops open. There was a gurgling sound and to his joy the fuel flowed freely out of the tanker, gushing down the incline and straight into the pond below. It was a big tanker and there was a lot of petrol. By now his head was bursting with pain but he fought against it.

To his dismay the fuel gauge on the outside of the vehicle showed that only half the fuel had decanted. There was nothing for it. Summoning up what energy he could and working against the migraine-like grip in
his head, he got into the driver's seat. He pointed the vehicle down the hill towards the pond and let the handbrake off. As it moved away, he opened the door and jumped out, falling roughly on his side.

The tanker careered down the rough track and he thought it would miss the water completely, but luck was on his side, and a large rock deflected the front wheels towards the target. It plunged into the floating scum at the edge of the pond with a loud splash.

The ground was wet with fuel. He felt in his pockets, then screamed with frustration. Just as he fell face down on the ground, exhausted, thinking all was lost, he felt a tap on his shoulder. It was James, aware of what Curtis was trying to do, holding out a small gas lighter. He grabbed it eagerly, moving them both back from the edge of the fuel-drenched ground. Then he found some dry grass to roll up into a ball, lit and threw it at the beginning of the fuel trail. There was a loud whoosh as the ground quickly ignited and a path of flame snaked downwards towards the pond, setting fire to adjacent grass and brush, eventually reaching the water, which then turned into a flaming surface. They stared at the inferno as it engulfed the half-submerged tanker. Minutes later it exploded and the whole area resembled a firestorm. Curtis and James were thrown to the ground by the blast.

To Curtis's surprise and relief, the pain in his ears subsided.

The days that followed were confusing. Miles Pinkerton's UFO theories were debunked, but he still maintained a naïve following. Rosalyn's body was never found, neither were those of missing persons or animals. The incident with the fuel tanker and setting fire to the pond was put down to mischievousness on the part of Curtis and James whilst under the influence of drink. The pond area was cordoned, and government scientists were working on the charred remains of plants and other samples but were not expected to reach any conclusions for some months.

Surprisingly, even though they had no answers, the scientists believed James's account of what happened. Security officials interviewed Curtis and James and it was carefully explained to them that if details of this situation leaked to the press, then all manner of cranks would appear on the scene and, worse, the public would panic. Every unexplained incident in the UK would be seen as a threat and chaos would ensue.

Curtis and James both agreed to accept, for form's sake and to ensure calm while government officers investigated the situation, a spurious police charge of mischievous behaviour. They would be bound over and given a suspended sentence by the local magistrate's court. James would later be found employment somewhere in the UK and Curtis agreed to be moved to a foreign newspaper where he would be able to make a career for himself under an assumed name. They were thanked for their bravery and would both be rewarded with a modest financial sum that would help them to start a new life.

It was all over.

The late autumn evening had been unusually bright in Northumberland, brighter than normal and, to everyone's delight, there was a trace of an aurora borealis, with bright lights flashing across the horizon, not normally seen this far south. It was a fantastic sight. The next day, a farmer gave his field the last plough of the season, ready for the winter to deal with the remaining clods of soil. As he drove his tractor up and down the furrows, alongside a narrow stream, a cloud of dust appeared to fall from the sky. He drove through it and sneezed as tiny seeds got into his nose. It was uncomfortable and his nose itched like crazy; he had to get home quickly to wash his face and deal with what felt like extreme hay fever.

The cloud of dust-like particles lay on the damp earth. Days later they seemed to move around like small worms, seeking crevices close to the stream.

They would sleep through the winter ready to germinate in spring.

13

The Dinner

John Adcock eased his arthritic limbs to the side of the taxi and squinted through the misty windows at the streets of York. His annual trip to the dinner was becoming more difficult the older he became, but as the organiser of the event he could hardly miss it. The taxi slowed outside an old building called Bedern Hall and a woman came out of the double doors with an umbrella unfolded, ready to shelter him inside.

"Madelaine, how nice to see you again."

Madelaine was in her middle fifties and had been responsible for organising the dinners when her predecessor had been taken ill. It was a responsible role, going well beyond the catering arrangements.

"Good to see you too, John. Come inside quickly, it's wet and horrible out here. I have some sad news, I'm afraid."

John wasn't surprised. He removed his coat in the hallway and accepted a cup of warm tea from a young steward.

Madelaine looked concerned. "We were expecting Alistair Strang and Michael Reaper. John, I'm sorry but

97

both men have been extremely sick. Alistair died three months ago and Michael only last week. That leaves..."

"I know, Madelaine, it's all right. None of us last forever. Let's get on with things, as best we can that is."

Madelaine smiled and touched his arm. She was fond of John. He had helped her look after her disabled son, by granting financial gifts that eased the burden enormously and she was forever grateful. It was this fact that focused her attention on the work of The Trust and the confidentiality that it demanded. It was a small duty to arrange a dinner once a year and she did it with gusto.

After visiting the rest room and adjusting his tie, John came into the dining room. He never regretted selecting Bedern Hall for the annual dinners for The Trust. It had an interesting history, dating from the late 1390s as a dining hall for the College of the Vicars Choral. It was prestigious and comfortable but above all, out of the way. That was to say, it was a long way from where most of the members of The Trust lived and worked, so ensuring their anonymity.

He surveyed the dinner table with its silverware and crystal glasses, the most striking feature being the special place settings that were appropriate to each of the members. It had always been set for all the members, even after they had passed on.

"Madelaine, the table is, as usual, absolutely perfect," he paused, "so it's just me then?"

"Yes, John, just you. Are you okay with...?"

`John interrupted saying softly, "Madelaine, my dear, I'm okay."

Madelaine left the room to arrange one place for dinner. John took a deep breath and walked around the table, smiling as he passed each of the twenty special place settings. They were indeed unique. Each setting had a small item in the middle of the place mat that appropriately fitted the member concerned.

A first edition of a novel belonged to James Coburn. He had been so pleased when he was finally published. The cash from the sales had been donated to The Trust. Alistair Strang's art brushes, amusingly crossed like ceremonial swords, were next in line. He had made a fortune painting a range of pictures including nude studies and this earned him ribald remarks from his fellows.

A barrister's wig, looking a bit crumpled after years of service, sat on a mat, a bit like a discarded bird's nest. It belonged to Jacob Trevain. He was a firebrand who championed the cases of people who could not afford legal services, as well as charging enormous sums of money to those who could. His was an easy nomination to the Trust. John paid homage to each place, stopping, and saying a quiet thank-you to men now long dead; men who had given so much and asked nothing in return.

Colin Redwood's parachute regiment beret and brigadier insignia almost filled all of one setting. His army exploits had provided extraordinary tales of courage and daring. His work mentoring young offenders had been exemplary. Alan Thomas's football boots were playfully kept with dry caked mud on them, and Madelaine refused to clean them. Alan had become a Premier League team manager and she teased him that he had a whole team to do jobs for him.

One place setting was the exception. On it was a bust, covered in a black cloth. This member, whose name was now never even mentioned, had disgraced The Trust. The man concerned was a photographer and had been tempted into the world of pornography. This was no great crime – tasteless but no more – until that is, he had dabbled with photographs of children. He was sent to prison. The Trust disowned him, but always set a place in this fashion, as a reminder of how far people can fall.

Passing this place mat always made John feel angry.

His mood brightened, though, when he moved on to that of his personal friend, Peter Brundle, whose setting was a rolled copy of his MPhil thesis on the Battle of Waterloo, splendid with a blue ribbon around it. Peter's infectious humour never failed to brighten John's mood even through terrible times, such as when his wife died of cancer. Some years ago, in a hotel in Hampshire, Peter was taken ill in his room; because of his age – and to be on the safe side – the ambulance crew decided to put him on a stretcher. As he was taken through the reception area and past the restaurant he sat bolt upright theatrically, and turned to concerned onlooking guests, saying, "It wasn't the food!" Just conjuring up Peter's face made John smile. Peter had been a Freemason and his setting was a pair of compasses and a square.

John finished his perambulations and took his place at the top of the table. He had hoped to say a few words to his remaining two members, but not now. He felt sad at their passing.

A young waitress served dinner, with Madelaine in attendance. It comprised a starter of smoked salmon, roast beef for the main course followed by a lemon posset. John raised his glass of claret in silent tribute to his friends.

As he put the wine glass back on the table, he recalled the heady days he enjoyed at Darwin College, Cambridge University in the late 1940s, with good friends, discussing the problems of the world One such lively debate involved John, Jacob, and Peter, after consuming copious amounts of wine.

The decade was a turbulent one. Markets had crashed before the war damaging investments and savings. Many of the upper and middle classes lost vast sums of money and were forced to seek employment or sell their assets. The economy, post-WWII, was in turmoil. Rebuilding the country threw people from all backgrounds together as they tried to reform their lives. Some people turned to communism, unaware of the evils of Stalin, and fascism remained rife in the east end of London, even after Hitler had been vanquished. A new socialist government worked against the odds to ensure equality and justice in all things, but war debts hampered their work.

John remembered that it was against this backdrop that enthusiastic discussions took place. What an intemperate and demonstrative youth he had been, full of the spirit of a *new dawn* for working people, jumping on a table shouting, "To arms friends, circumstances are raping our lives. Are we to sit by and let our neighbours suffer? Have we no hearts, do we care so little?" It was later, in more sober mood that reasonable discourse took place, and The Trust was formed.

The aim was simple: they would seek to provide funds to those in dire need. Members were recruited from within their own circle or by recommendation and each had to have large incomes or access to substantial savings. The purpose of The Trust was made abundantly clear to all who joined. They would give regular payments from their earnings and also raise funds from contacts including the City of London – which proved the most lucrative source. Above all, it was their collective values of social fairness and honesty that bound them in friendship and benevolence.

Membership reached twenty with others maintaining no more than a passing association. The projects they subscribed to were varied in nature. The Trust remained secretive in its work, untrusting of a world suspicious of altruism and which disbelieved the fact that charitable deeds could be done without wanting something in return.

After his dinner, John sipped his port and sank back in his chair, pleasant memories swirling in his mind. Madelaine silently served him coffee and left him to his thoughts.

All of a sudden, John began to hear Grieg's piano concerto in A minor, a piece of music that his wife Hannah loved so much. He still felt the pain of her passing. As his eyes clouded with tears at the thought of her, he became aware that the room was becoming hazy. To his astonishment, he saw his erstwhile friend Peter standing to his left.

"Peter, you old son of a gun, is that you?"

"Yes, old fruit, 'tis me. You're putting on weight, Mr Podge!"

"Ever complimentary, Peter. But...how are you...?"

"Don't ask questions," Peter replied laughing.

John felt so good in his company; it was like old times – such camaraderie and humour. How he missed his friends.

"Who squashed my blasted wig, bloody buffoons," said another voice on his left. It had to be Jacob

"Not me, Jacob," said John eagerly, "there are too many fleas in it to chance my touch!"

John was beaming now. He heard a tinny echo of men laughing heartily and recognised it as Colin and Alan. They chided Jacob and suggested that his baldness would have made it difficult to keep a wig on, to which Jacob shouted genial abuse about pretentious authors and dull historians. More voices followed and John found himself a mere spectator in a cacophony of laughter. It enveloped him, it embraced him, and it filled him with joy.

Then there was silence. Through the misty air he saw his colleagues now seated at the table, staring at him all smiling as if waiting for him to open proceedings. It was a pleasant, cheerful sight.

Peter stood up and smiled broadly at him, then he held out his arms. Slowly, the others did too, beckoning him to join them. John felt elated and so incredibly happy. He stood, walked to the right of the table, and approached his friends. He touched the hands of the first group and felt a tingle in their handshakes.

As he shook the last hand, he slowly looked over his shoulder and saw himself in the chair at the head of the table, head lolled to one side, quite still.

He understood perfectly and felt no fear or dread. Then he turned and joined his friends as they walked into a thickening mist.

14

Digging

Thump, thump. I force my spade into the earth, mercilessly slicing the yielding soil and crunching the stone. I despise that sound now. As if pleading for its life the dark, sticky soil clings to the spade. Alice likes dark earth and always wants potatoes to be planted. I said she must be Irish, and she didn't like that; she said it was rude and unfair to say such things. That's Alice for you. She's always fair. I miss her every day.

I must keep to the straight line and dig deep. The early morning mist is long gone, and the autumn sun is low on the horizon, trying to shake itself from the wet misty shroud that embraces it.

Thump, thump. The sound continues and my shoulder hurts with each blow, but I must keep going. Every time I hit a stone, sparks fly, and I think of a friend no longer with me. How easily they go. After an hour with sparks from flints jousting with my spade, I lose concentration and my mind wanders. To politicians, kings, and bishops. Alice said that it was people like them that made me link potatoes with the Irish, the ugly use of prejudice together with creative political selfishness. They dispense rudeness to shore up their superiority. She's smart. No schooling as such, just plain honest common sense.

Thump, thump. I try to link each spark with one of the nameless elites, as well as friends now gone. I'm up to fifty sparks now and can still find room for more tags to each one. How sad. Sod the king, the vote-for-me brigade and the "our father in heaven" bunch; they're the ones to blame. No damned common sense like my Alice. No "love thy neighbour" or sense of humanity, nor sense of when "enough is enough". Another spark from a flint; I think I'll give up counting lost friends – it only makes me angry. I do miss Alice and just want to see her again – soon.

Thump, thump. My arms and shoulders tire and not for the first time I am tempted to rest. I bet the kings, politicians and bishops don't get this tired. So tired yet unable to stop. I focus my strength and dig straight and deep. Don't think about "why", it doesn't help, just survive the day; survive this odd and arbitrary business of doing as I am told.

Thump, thump. I hit the earth again and it reminds me of that familiar thump, thump, which makes the earth shake and strikes fear into us all. Whatever did I do to the man that causes that thump? Is he a king, a politician, or a bishop? No, of course not, they are just instruments of the elite; they don't know me, but are told to kill me, using their machines that move more earth per thump than my pathetic spade. I bet they ask the same questions of me as I of them.

After four hours my spade has taken me long and deep across the wasted earth, the cut edges speckled with broken flint-stones flashing in the light. Eerily, I imagine that on each one of them there is a picture of a friend or some passing soldier I once knew, as well as those of kings, politicians, and bishops. It's an illusory moment, thinking of them all buried together, their lives remembered in a pictorial arcade of death. How much longer? How much deeper?

Then the Regimental Sergeant Major stands above me. "Now then, son," he says, kindlier than he has ever spoken. "Stop now, you need do no more."

I ask him why and he replies like a schoolmaster. "Because it's all over at eleven minutes past eleven," and he taps his watch.

I look back at the well-dug trench, fashioned for war, right up until the very second of its cessation.

"Then, why this...?"

He replies guardedly and in a manner that sums it all up. "Because we just couldn't trust them."

Tears fall across my mud-stained face and glisten against my skin - I slide down against the side of the muddy trench.

He turns to go and adds in a matter-of-fact way, "But it's all over now, it's peace again."

Which one of the kings, politicians or bishops finally shouted loud enough for it to all stop? No matter, I will soon see Alice again and the next time I will be digging, it will be for potatoes.

15

Interstellar Highway

Giles closed the door to his cottage with a bang and strode purposefully down the path, slamming the gate equally loudly as he left the garden. *Bloody women!* he thought angrily. It had been agreed that he could watch an international rugby match at Twickenham, but the addition of an unscripted celebration with the lads after a stunning win against the French had been too much for his partner Helen. A dried-up supper and the dead ashes in the fireplace were evidence of his expected return at an appointed hour.

His efforts to explain that it could hardly have been avoided failed miserably, though inwardly he regretted overlooking the need to telephone her, and it all ended up as a kind of verbal car crash with both parties calling up trivial incidents to bolster their positions. Helen stormed to bed and Giles decided to go for a drive.

Putting both arms on the roof of his red convertible, a 1995 Lancia sports car, he took a deep breath, exhaling the warm mist into the frosty night air. The weekend had taken a turn for the worse and he was forced to admit that it could have been predicted. Helen was the sweetest person in the world and yet, beyond today's faux pas, their egos sometimes collided; when this happened, the effect was volcanic. Perhaps it was inevitable. Each had travelled the route from mid-twenties to just over thirty, establishing their lives professionally, he as a lawyer and she as an English teacher, rationalism versus romanticism.

He put his leather overnight bag into the boot, opened the car door and sat down heavily in the sports seat; the rainwater from the soft-top splashed his face and he brushed it aside irritably. The leather upholstery felt cold, but he was beyond caring and threw his coat onto the small back seat. He sat still for a moment, then threw caution to the wind and reached for a small tin box in the glove compartment that contained several roll-up cigarettes. It wasn't the wisest thing to do but lighting up cannabis was what he now really craved. Old university habits die hard. As he inhaled the soothing aromatic smoke, he noticed the bedroom light in the cottage go out. Smoke filled his lungs, and he held it there for a brief moment before exhaling – it felt good.

The spliff softened his anger. He felt silly walking out in a huff and was only too aware that he could be impetuous. He reasoned that she expected too much from him and for his part he took her too much for granted. There was a strong bond between them, and he loved Abigail without question. But in situations like today, when tension rose out of control, he needed space to cool down.

He finished the cannabis cigarette, threw the butt into the road, and turned the key in the ignition, and the engine burst into life. It had a powerful yet soft rumble to it, displaying strength of engineering with the subtlety of Italian sex appeal. As the car pulled away, Giles took out his mobile telephone and put it into the special holder on the mahogany dashboard – it flashed brightly as it received a small charge of electricity. The tyres skidded on the gravel as the car sought traction then, gripping the surface, the

Lancia accelerated gracefully, and he felt a tantalising force in the middle of his back as it picked up speed.

He planned to take a shortcut from Fetcham to the M25 motorway. This meant travelling via small, narrow roads just about wide enough for one and a half cars. Tonight, the trees either side of the road seemed to dip inwards, eerily reaching towards the car.

Having to keep his speed down irritated him and he regretted not taking the longer route via the main road. To make matters worse there was a thickening mist that almost obscured the lanes ahead. It was almost midnight and he planned to drive for about an hour, cool down and then head home. Eventually, he was relieved to see a dimly lit blue and white sign indicating the direction to the M25 and he turned down the slip road and onto the motorway. As soon as he got onto the M25 he settled down for the short drive to the junction for the A3 to take a circular route past Wisley Gardens to the cottage. The Lancia felt good, and his hands caressed the wooden steering wheel. He always felt relaxed in this car.

All of a sudden, he felt a strange, throbbing headache come on and regretted the puffs of cannabis. It was so bad that he considered stopping briefly, but it was late, and he thought better of it. The headache passed and as it did so, the mist took on a strange hazy, bright blue-purple tinge and he noticed that from time to time there were small flares of light as though somebody was taking flash photographs. Narrow coloured beams of light sporadically flashed then exploded like starburst fireworks. Bemused, Giles thought it was the result of an expensive birthday party celebration.

Unperturbed, his thoughts returned to his personal situation. Giles was very much the realist, wanting quick solutions, sticking to the rules and a clear focus. On the other hand, Helen lived in a classical world of paper tigers, drama, and literature, and wouldn't see a charging elephant until she felt it breathing on her neck, and even then, she would probably offer it a bun. How could you get mad with such a person? He felt remorseful and berated himself for being so hard-headed at times, and even began to question his manner towards her. He jerked his head to one side, as if waking from a day-dream – it takes two to change, why the heck should he do all the work?

"Oh, why do you make me so mad!" he said to himself.

Suddenly he saw a car undertaking on the inside lane. That irritated him immensely and he looked up to catch the driver's eye in order to give him or her, an admonishing glare; he flinched with fright.

The car was a large red American Buick with lots of shiny chrome and ostentatious fins on the back. Driving it was a man wearing a large white cowboy hat with silver studs around the centre. His whole body was hunched over the wheel as though he was concentrating hard on just driving straight ahead. It was bizarre.

As Giles strained to get a better view the driver looked up. His chest instantly tightened at the sight of a heavily creased, green-tinged face with blazing red eyes and a large bulbous nose. The Buick driver then turned his attention back towards the road ahead and accelerated into the distance. Giles shook his head. Was he fantasising? Was that real? It must surely be a man in fancy dress.

Giles tried to make sense of the fleeting image. He didn't feel scared, just incredulous, as he watched the rear lights of the large vehicle disappear into the distance.

Blinking a few times, he peered through the rain and mist. The Buick seemed to be jet propelled, it travelled so fast.

There were more flashes of light, from the left, right, and sometimes high in the sky. He began to feel irritable. Where was the A3 junction? He had been driving for ages and yet had seen no signs whatever. Something was distinctly wrong.

His mobile telephone flashed and before he could reach for it the speaker came on automatically; a strange high-pitched voice, with an American twang and a strange echo addressed him.

"Good evening, you are approaching junction twenty-three on the interstellar highway. You cannot take this junction. Please drive carefully. Thank you."

"What the...?" he blurted. "How...?"

His heart beat faster as a junction appeared and he tried to turn the steering wheel to leave the motorway, but it wouldn't budge.

"Damned wheel, turn you bastard, turn," he yelled in frustration.

Even the accelerator and brake were inoperable. He felt an unaccustomed helplessness overwhelm him. This was crazy.

Suddenly, a silver-grey bullet shaped car overtook him like a rocket. His speedometer was showing eighty-five miles an hour, so what speed was that car doing?

Gripping the steering wheel tightly he tried to concentrate on the situation. What on earth was happening? He was powerless in a car that wouldn't respond; his car, his Lancia, perfectly serviced with a clear MOT just didn't behave like that.

As if all that was not crazy enough, his eyes widened in surprise and shock when, completely out of nowhere he came upon a dozen American Bison running in front of him in the same direction. On top of two of them sat Sioux Indians in full-feathered headdress.

This was too much, and he tried to pull the steering wheel hard to the left, then the right. This time the car responded, but his hands clenched tightly as he narrowly missed hitting the large beasts. When he eventually began to overtake them, he noticed the bison had red bloodshot eyes and saliva was falling from their mouths in great white globules – they must have been travelling at least at sixty miles an hour, how could this be?

The Sioux Indians, like the driver of the large Buick earlier, were hunched forward oblivious to anything but following the highway ahead. Their faces were contorted, and they concentrated hard on the task of driving their bison forward.

Giles was incredulous. Was there a circus in the area? Were they all high on drugs or something? This was a nightmare – he would never, ever, touch cannabis again. He drove on past the bison at high speed, through the mist and rain, accompanied by flashes of light, this time orange and green.

Fidor laughed as he looked at the screen and glimpsed Giles's shocked face. He sat in a large high-backed swivel chair, dwarfed within a cavernous area on a deserted asteroid, Star 4305. The area was the size of the Albert Hall and was surrounded by large metal cabinets covered with lights, flashing screens, pulsing nuclear and solar energy cells, cables, and wires. A three-D image of Giles appeared on a large screen high up on the wall in front of him. He enjoyed frightening creatures from around the universe and his personally constructed interstellar highway was the best sport he had developed in a hundred timespans.

He chuckled at the antics of the American Indians riding the Bison. That was funny, very funny, but not at all like the time that he had twenty elephants bumping into cars and trucks with their mahouts atop them; they had been crouched in eternal fear, each whipping his beast for all he was worth, destined to ride the highway in perpetuity, their bodies rotting and flesh falling off but the skeletons remaining fixed to their mission. He was especially proud of that construct but was sad that the elephants had long since run themselves out, tiring and eventually being bumped off the highway by speeding vehicles.

Then his head jerked forwards as someone slapped the nape of his neck hard. He looked up in surprise.

"Fidor, so this is what you have been up to," said his sister Granya. "I've been watching for the last timespan, and I don't like what I see. You're a cruel man Fidor, just like the Federation said, but I didn't know you had created anything like this."

Fidor rubbed his neck and smiled at Granya.

"Dearest sister, when our parents allowed us to stay on planet Orama—" he paused as she interjected furiously.

"No Fidor. They exiled you, then me, because I am your sister remember?"

She glared at him.

"Yes, alright, alright, have it your way, exiled. But we have all we need here and to all intents and purposes we are able to do as we please. And I have all this marvelous equipment to play with. I have so much fun."

He waved his arms at the array of equipment, screens, and lights around him and laughed again.

Granya was not impressed and pressed home her anger.

"But it's cruel and that's why you were sent here, Fidor. You never change, do you? If Mador finds out, you will be in big trouble."

"He won't, dear sister, he won't. Now sit down and enjoy the show."

Fidor turned his attention to the screen and pointed a long bony finger at the image of Giles. "I particularly like this group of creatures. They are intelligent, very intelligent and they possess an enormous amount of emotion. This means that they are brave and courageous but, on the other hand, so much more easily frightened and easily angered. It is so funny, isn't it?"

Granya screwed her face up and bit her green lip. She had watched the earlier manoeuvre to transfer the hapless creature Giles from the M25 to the interstellar highway from behind a large cabinet in the corner, near the screen on the wall and realised what Fidor was up to. She despised her brother but hated the ancient rules that had shackled her to his exile even more. She looked up at the screen and felt sick at his antics.

Giles saw the mobile telephone flash again. It came on and a voice with high-pitched American twang spoke.

"Good evening, you are approaching junction twenty-four on the interstellar highway. You cannot take this junction. Please drive carefully. Thank you."

He raised his hand to his forehead, pinched the top of his nose as if to bring him back to some kind of consciousness. He was sweating profusely, his hands felt clammy on the steering wheel and his feet had long since left the pedals as the car seemed to speed on regardless.

As he tried to make sense of the utter madness, a bright light appeared on his right. To his horror he saw a battered saloon car in which a cadaverous figure of an elderly man was sprawled back in his seat. His skin was yellow and taut against his skull, and his eyes were bulging. Wisps of remaining hair on his almost bald head stuck out untidily from the sides. The only sign that he was breathing was the white frothy bubbles that dripped profusely from the corners of his mouth. As Giles stared at him, the figure slowly turned and looked at him.

His forlorn, helpless expression begged for help. Powerless, Giles could only return his gaze to the road ahead as his vehicle accelerated away. He desperately searched for a way out, a junction, – yet knew that he didn't have control if one appeared!

Giles called on his inner strength; he was not one to give in easily – it wasn't his way. It was time to keep calm and think.

He reached for the mobile telephone and took it off the cradle. As he pressed the pre-set code for Abigail, it lit up and made him jump.

"This is the interstellar control. You are not allowed to contact anyone whilst on the interstellar highway. Please drive ahead and enjoy your journey. Thank you."

He held the phone close to his mouth and shouted. "Stop. You. Idiot. I want to talk."

The mobile telephone remained live, but no voice replied. He convinced himself that he had made an impact on the voice and continued.

"What's going on, are you controlling my car?"

There was only silence.

"If I am dreaming this, then I will wake up and flush you down the toilet. If I am not and this is some kind of nightmarish situation which you are controlling, I'm here to tell you that you are a freak, you're pathetic, warped, do you understand me?"

He was angry and shouting, then slammed the phone back in the holder. It flashed for an instant then went out.

Granya heard the whole exchange from the back of the hall where she was hidden in the shadows. She was glad that she hadn't been with Fidor when Giles shouted at him. When someone got the better of him, he lost control of himself and that was always dangerous. That was why he was exiled. He had been considered dangerous to himself and to others in the community.

She had a slim chance to change things. Opening a small bag in front of her she brought out a round stone about three inches in diameter, opaque and speckled with brightness like a fire opal. It shimmered brightly and piercing coloured shafts of light shot out from its surface. This was her only hope. It had been given to her by Mador and was to be used only in extreme situations. First of all, she needed to get outside the metallic building, with its nuclear and solar power influences, to be able to use the stone effectively.

She would do it. It had to be done.

Meanwhile, Fidor laughed nervously and fidgeted with his controls.

"Male hell-creature. So, you insult your controller, do you? Well now, you will regret that," he spat in anger.

Far behind him Granya was running into the darkness, between the tall metallic cabinets covered in flashing lights, her diaphanous robe flowing, tiny shards of light escaping from the round stone she clasped tightly in her fist.

Giles squinted into the mist and rain and closed his eyes when flashes of light shot left and right. The car was cool, but he still felt hot. His fingers were beginning to grip the wheel so tightly it made his knuckles white. Then it dawned on him that he too was beginning to hunch over the steering wheel and quickly forced himself to sit up straight and avoid the crouch position.

He would not be cowed.

Unable to understand what was happening ate into Giles. Here was something over which he had no control. It was like when Helen did not understand him; then he paused and corrected himself. Perhaps he expected too much and needed to understand her a bit more.

However, at the moment he was so angry and just wanted to get to the person behind the voice on his mobile telephone and rip his throat out.

Two vehicles shot past the Lancia startling him – they narrowly missed the car's bonnet and then weaved left and right into the distance. Moments later he only just avoided two tall, thin, human-like figures meandering along the middle of the highway, holding their heads in despair. Pumping the brake had no effect at all, even when he tried to get the vehicle to slow down using the gears, it wouldn't respond.

Looking around he could see more vehicles coming towards his rear. In a small Mini Cooper on his left side, four skeletons rattled around the interior of the vehicle as it careered ahead at breakneck speed. One of the skeletons wore a baseball cap that had fallen forward and obscured one of the eye sockets giving it an incongruous, jaunty appearance.

On his right, seconds later, a Mercedes saloon swerved about as the driver, a woman with a crazed look on her face was trying to climb out of the car window. An unseen force seemed to restrain her, and she was screaming madly and pulling at her hair. Her face was contorted with fear, and she seemed oblivious to the danger, concerned only with vacating the box prison of her vehicle. At one point she reached out and touched the side of the Lancia, her nails making a faint scratching sound – suddenly the Mercedes slowed and skewed off the road. There was a loud noise and a flash of explosive light.

Giles was really worried – would that eventually happen to him? No matter whether he crouched and drove for an eternity or fought back, was this to be his destiny?

The mobile phone flashed and the voice came on again.

"Good evening, you are approaching junction twenty-five on the interstellar highway. You cannot take this junction. Please drive carefully. Thank you."

"Warped pig, bastard, mindless fool..." Giles shouted madly.

To his surprise he felt good shouting at the unseen nightmarish force. Being powerless is one thing but giving that all-important "V" sign in the face of terrible adversity, like a brave soldier about to be beheaded, sat very neatly with him. He took his hands off the wheel and put them to his head. Why not? Sod it. The car would not divert from its track.

Was it his imagination, or did he hear someone laughing?

A blaze of light appeared in the rear-view mirror. A vehicle was behind him and flashing its lights wildly. He could do no more than try to see through the light to make out the danger. Astonishingly, the lights dimmed, and the vehicle started to overtake. It slowed alongside and as he looked up, he recoiled in horror. The vehicle was a large sedan with shiny silver fenders front and back shaped to look like teeth. Inside the sedan sat a large, fat, shapeless, green-fleshed creature, so big that the arms appeared short and squat against its frame that almost filled the vehicle.

There was no discernible neck and the head seemed squashed into the body. The creature's face had pieces of green flesh hanging from it and the eyeballs protruded so much that they looked as though they would almost fall out. There was no noticeable mouth or nose. It looked straight at him, and he felt its burning repulsive gaze. His courage almost deserted him. This was too much.

The vehicle dropped back and then flashed its lights as it accelerated towards the Lancia. It would surely hit him. Closer and closer it came until eventually it bumped into the back of the car. His heart skipped a beat; was he going to be killed? The sedan seemed to be positioning itself for another shunt.

As his heart beat faster and he braced himself for more to come, the mobile telephone flashed, and he heard the voice with an American accent.

"Good evening, you are approaching junction twenty-six on the interstellar highway. You cannot..."

Then, surprisingly, the American voice was abruptly cut short.

After a short silence, a female voice, calmer and softer said, "...you can take the next junction, repeat, you can take the next junction, please do so quickly and drive carefully."

Giles's spirits rose in an instant and he didn't need telling twice. As he peered through the falling rain, mist and flashing coloured lights he saw a junction come into view. A neon sign with the word, "Here" ringed in flashing lights indicated the turnoff and he turned the steering wheel. It responded easily and so did the brake when he touched it to slow down. The large sedan with its green monster driver overtook and sped past.

The small slip road turned sharply to the left and he had to reduce speed in order not to slide off the road. His hopes of freedom were rising, and he felt the elation of a prisoner being let free from a cell.

Soon he was back on a normal country road and for a time his body shook with relief at the normality of it all. His mind was numb. He slowed the Lancia to take a bend and noticed a small lay-by, into which he instinctively turned and stopped. After cranking on the handbrake, he turned off the engine, stared ahead and put his head on the steering wheel. Although his fingers could hardly work properly, he sent a quick text message to Abigail, to say he was safe and not to worry and that he loved her. It was impossible to drive further. He was utterly exhausted, and he reached into the back of the car for the car blanket and his coat and settled down to sleep.

The sun was well above the horizon when Giles awoke from a lengthy stupor, feeling enormously refreshed and surprisingly clear-headed. The drive home was uneventful, and he felt strangely calm as the morning sun began to warm the car. He reached home, parked, and went inside just as Helen was preparing breakfast. He reached out to her, and she gladly fell into his arms. He said sorry, she said sorry, and they held each other tightly, reflecting together on the pointless exchanges of the previous night.

Giles wanted to tell Helen that he had smoked cannabis the night before and about the terrible horrific dream, for that was what it must have surely been. But it all seemed so very stupid, so stupid that he would be certified insane if he told anyone – it was so irrational, who would believe him? Besides, he had better things to think about than a stupid dream; he grabbed Helen again and kissed her tenderly, then led her upstairs.

Later, Giles collected his overnight bag from the Lancia and made sure the doors were locked. As he did so, something caught his eye. It was a small dent in the rear bumper and several flakes of silvery paint were attached to the surface. He reached down to wipe the flecks away and surprisingly they turned to dust as he brushed them off with his hand. Pride would prevent him from mentioning the bump to Helen, so he thought it better to ignore it.

Granya sat with an elder as he tried to undo the damage of countless timespans by reprogramming equipment and shutting down power systems. However, one programme was kept very much operational. She had taken the only action possible although it went against her beliefs and the rules of family, but it had had to be done. Her eyes were full of tears as she looked up at the screen and saw her brother in a large grey and badly dented Cadillac. Fidor was sitting in the rear with half a dozen cadaverous creatures pawing at his face and body, as the vehicle careered at speed along an interstellar highway, through rain, mist and flashing lights, swerving around the debris of abandoned and crashed vehicles.

His eyes were bulging, and he was screaming, but no one could hear his voice.

16

Deadly Habit

It's getting very difficult to focus, I can hardly move, and this looks like the end. I just don't understand. Why me? For goodness' sake, there must be standards in life; if you let things go, then trouble follows, and it all gets so complicated - my dad reasoned that one out and behaved accordingly. It worked for him. You have to be strong - it's no good mewling about the softness of women, they know what they are doing and frankly, some of them get away with murder. So, when my partner goes on a bit, and for God's sake, she knows the consequences, then I must take positive action. Then it stops and we get back to normal - so that's all there is to it.

That's what happened tonight. She went on and on. Why they do that I don't know - it must be some kind of death wish injected into that gender at birth. So, I slapped. Okay, more than once, but she did try to hit me after all. As usual there were tears. Afterwards, things usually get back to normal, all lovey dovey and lots of *'I'm sorry...'* Then we would hit the sack and the old magic does the trick. But not this time.

What in God's name was so special about tonight? Yes, I drew blood, but it wasn't my fault, my signet ring did that. I got her antiseptic but that was just thrown at the wall - so much for gratitude. If that's the way she wants it this time, I'll leave out the sex – that's her loss. I thought that would teach her a lesson, but apparently not.

Going onto the veranda overlooking the forest covered in an early thick white frost seemed like a good idea. I wanted to calm the anger, let the heart stop beating so hard and regain a sense of perspective – I certainly wasn't going to get any in the bedroom. Perhaps it wasn't the best thing to do in a flimsy bathrobe, but I thought it would be like the Scandinavians do, get kind of sauna-hot then dash out into the cold to revitalise the body and concentrate the mind. Heaven knows I needed to concentrate.

When I turned, the damned balcony door had shut and being of a particular security design there is no handle on the outside. I banged hard on the glass, very hard. My partner staggers into the lounge and sees me and is all very theatrical, dabbing her bruises and holding her cut lip – it was really only a small cut. I appeal for her to open the door and it falls on deaf ears. That woman is mentally ill. She sits on the corner of the couch, just looking at me – no sign of recognition, or the danger I am in. She just has a dull, spiteful look in her eyes.

I ask nicely for her to open the goddamned door. I plead with her, which is certainly not easy for me, you understand. When that brings no success, I bang hard again on the windowpane, but its security strength holds fast, but my hands are by now quite numb. I then resort to telling her all the good things I have done for her and how damned lucky she is. But there's still no response – she just sits there as if in a trance. I truly wonder what I saw in her. I cannot fathom the ingratitude. Selfish, neurotic woman.

The cold is now unbearable, and I am beginning to feel drowsy. I have no fear; fear needs a heartbeat and I suspect mine is barely discernible. She still stares at me and is now crying. If she is so upset, why the hell doesn't she let me in? I crawl to the glass doors to the balcony to get close to the clear surface to see if I can get some warmth, but no joy, it is worse because the glass is icy cold. I cannot shout any more, my voice will not work.

I don't understand why this is happening. What did I do that was that bad?

You give someone the very best in life, and yes, sometimes, like my dad perhaps you go a little too far. But a slap is a slap, it's not like murder – so why this? It's been a little frequent lately, I know, but she makes me so mad – it's her fault not mine, she makes me do it. I know that it mustn't become a habit, but "needs must" if we are to be a perfect partnership. She has to learn.

Perhaps I can change my style, although I'm now beginning to fear the worst. As I look through my clouded vision and I see with horror that she is still crying and has a bottle of pills in her hand. She's opening the top and looks at me through tear-stained eyes.

Don't do it, stupid cow!

She tips the lot into her mouth.

It becomes clear to me now - it's all over.

17

Shiva's Hand

Some men are naturally happy, and this radiates from within. For others, unhappiness cleaves to them as if the result of an injury, so deep and painful that it is impossible to treat; mortally wounding their spirit. That was how it was with Mike Chandler. Despite enjoying good health and the enduring love of his daughter, Hermione, the itch in his soul from his wife's wasting death from cancer five years previous consumed him. He dismissed his daughter's approaches to talk things over with hurtful detachment, and there was a degree of fraudulence in his assertions that work required his attention.

So, everybody was surprised when Hermione persuaded him to join her on a trip to Goa. On arrival, Mike was fazed by the chaotic driving and continuous honking of horns as well as wandering cows.

In the hotel bar that night Hermione said. 'Okay, Pops, I fancy a bit of culture. Look at these brochures, we should go to the vast ruins at Hampi, it's a UNESCO World Heritage site, it dates from the fourteenth century Vijayanagara era.'

Mike began to close his eyes.

'I'm losing you, aren't I? No matter, we're going and that's that.' She smiled defiantly. 'Okay," he replied, 'as long as there are no more bloody cows!'

The next day they set off for Hampi. The resulting train experience, with crowded carriages, persistent loud calls from chai sellers and interesting toilets, strained Mike's patience. After settling into their hotel, a guide called Rakesh arranged transport for the next day.

At Hampi, they walked amongst the ruins, and Rakesh told Hermione about the Hindu religion, explaining the principal deities, often known as the trinity of gods, Brahma, Vishnu, and Shiva.

Mike raised his eyebrows.

Rakesh continued patiently. 'Brahma was born in a lotus flower, is half man and half woman and is central to the beginning of mankind. Vishnu is the god of mercy and goodness and detests ego. Shiva is widely revered in India and is the destroyer of evil, but in a simpler explanation, sir, he also destroys ego and bad things, opening up the path for new creation. He is about letting go of things that are bad or don't work. He may be called the destroyer, but he represents spirituality and is central to meditation, helping us all to look beyond ourselves to create a blissful state of existence.'

Hermione was enthralled. Eventually, they came to the Sasivekala Ganesha Temple. Inside was an enormous statue.

'This is the god Ganesha,' explained Rakesh proudly. 'He is the offspring of Shiva.'

'Looks like an elephant,' intoned Mike dismissively.

'Indeed, sir, but look at every detail of the statue.'

Rakesh earnestly explained the importance of each element of the god. 'Ganesh stood upon a mouse, which transported him around. The mouse identifies with ego – keep it small and yet strong. The broken left tusk is about emotions and the need to recognise them for the imposters that they are, whereas the full tusk indicates wisdom, which should be used judiciously. The two large ears note the need to listen carefully. His spiritual presence is meant to remove obstacles and ensure success. That is good, yes?'

Mike grunted disagreeably, removed his hat, and wiped away the sweat – only four days left.

Hermione gave him a look that defied him to say anything rude.

Later, they set off to Sunset Point in a traditional tuk-tuk. The road was steep and bumpy, and Hermione hooted with playful alarm.

Mike recalled days like this with Alison, her laugh and mischievous smile. That was before his house of cards crumbled in the face of cruel disease. His heart slowly shattered as he watched her die. Then nothing. Emptiness. That awful total and complete loss.

Mike got out of the tuk-tuk and wondered if his joints would ever recover. The path to the top of the hill led through a stone archway towards a courtyard at a small temple.

Hermione was bubbling, 'Hey, Pops, look at the sun, it's huge. Let's go, before it drops out of sight."

She ran towards the ridge. As Mike walked past the corner of the temple a man emerged from nearby rocks. His near naked body was covered in what looked like white ash and his hair was long and matted like his beard. A vivid blue stain encompassed his throat, and he held a wooden staff. It was as though he was staring directly into Mile's soul. It felt uncanny. He looked away quickly and strode to the top of the hill.

Joining Rakesh, he said unsteadily. 'Who was that nearly naked chap back there?'

Rakesh looked at him warily. 'Sir, he was Sadhu, a holy man, whose sole purpose is to pray and be in touch with the gods. The detaches himself from the material world and owns nothing, relying on the charity from the community. It is said Sadhus have strange powers. They will often be asked for predictions. When angered they have even been known to curse people. Is there anything wrong?"

'No, thank goodness,' replied Mike, unconvincingly.

The three of them watched the magnificent sunset in silence. As they later drove off, Mike looked back and was startled to see the dark silhouette of the Sadhu looking after him.

Back in the hotel at Benaulim, Hermione and Mike argued when she unwisely tried to get him to a attend a meditation session. She felt he needed to relax, but he resented being told and shouted at her. Mike brooded on his bad behaviour, apologised, and urged her to enjoy the remainder of the holiday alone.

He planned to spend the next few days in his room. After a Thali supper, he drank several glasses of whisky and fell asleep. On waking, his mouth felt sticky, and his head was fuzzy. An intense fragrance of incense surprised him and staring at the whiteness of the curtain he saw the unmistakable shape of a woman appearing through a thick mist.

He sat bolt upright. 'Alison?'

'Mike.' She said, smiling beautifully as she always did. 'You're getting angry, my love, and that won't do. We discussed it all, remember? Don't let anger overcome you, deal with the inevitable, move on, don't be alone. Just remember all our precious moments, love me forever but get on with life - you are doing anything but that.'

'I know, but...' his voice faltered.

'Now none of your *buts*. You were always so good at that. We talked it over in my last weeks and agreed. Look at you now, darling. Almost an awkward misanthrope and exceedingly angry.'

Mike knew in his heart it was true.

To his horror Alison's shape started to change, imperceptibly at first. It laughed and in a strange tinny voice not at all like Alison's, said, 'You find it difficult to listen to reason. You need to have two big ears, like me.'

The ears began to get bigger, and a large trunk grew from the face, the body also got larger as it took on the Hindu god-like form of Ganesha.

Mike was enraged, 'You're not Alison. How do you know these personal things? You trespass on her memory, on my grief. How dare you, get out, go! You're no more than a stupid vision created from indigestion. Just go!'

Ganesha turned away. 'I am unable to help you, Mike, and that makes me very unhappy.'

Mike cursed again. 'Get out, ugly beast, get out of my mind.'

The apparition disappeared. When the mist cleared, another figure appeared. It was a regal looking man around whose blue coloured neck lay a coiled snake, and in the middle of his forehead was a bright third eye. White ash smeared his body and his hair, giving him the appearance of a dishevelled ghost. He wore a headdress surmounted by a crescent moon and brandished a trident. He snarled at Mike through menacing blood-red lips.

'The Sadhu was right. You lack emotion and you must find it. I am Shiva. As for Ganesha, he is my offspring whom you deign to call an ugly beast.'

He pointed the trident directly at Mike and his third eye glowed. 'You are the ugly beast. You can be saved, but only you can make it work.'

A swirling wind encircled Mike and Shiva gripped his right arm tightly. Up into the inky black sky they went, circling and twisting until he felt sick. The air felt cold against his face, and he was frightened. Suddenly, he found himself standing on enormous pages of printed numbers. He walked across them, with his hands on his head.

'What the hell...?'

'You surely recognise this – it's your company's financial figures, enough to blot out the world. You stick your head into them, and they shroud you – your solace. They're your emotional blinkers. You see nothing else. But people preoccupied with their own affairs do nothing for others - we can change all that.'

Shiva produced an enormous axe and chopped furiously at the pages until they were completely shredded.

Mike looked on incredulously.

'Now more,' shouted Shiva, and he produced for a burning torch.

Mike's Factory came into view, and he screamed as Shiva started to set fire to it.

'No, don't do this...please,' he shouted.

Shiva put his face close to Mike's. 'I am the destroyer, Mike, don't you remember the description of me? I break things down. I will do this to the very things that prevent you from living a normal life. This is my role, and I am really rather good at it.'

Mike watched helplessly as flames consumed the buildings and screamed obscenities at Shiva who was unmoved at his pleas. He fell through the air, down towards the earth, to the cool sheets of his bed. His face was wet with tears. When he opened his eyes, Shiva was standing imperiously above him.

'To destroy is not wrong if it leads to something better being constructed in its place that avoids the mistakes and pain of the past. Heed this, Mike. It's up to you now.'

There was a loud ringing in Mike's head and all the angry grief-laden comments he had ever made crowded his mind

Four months after their return home Hermione received an invitation from her father whom she had not see since the Goa holiday. It was to attend the reopening of the Treadwell Factory. On arrival, she gasped with surprise. The gates had been rebuilt in an ornately patterned black metal and a white tiled path led to the front door. Two small fountains bubbled in the middle of the grassed areas.

The deputy manager greeted her. 'Hermione so nice to see you. What did you do to your father? He's so relaxed about everything despite the fire. The workforce has been retained and there's a tremendous sense of harmony. Its a miracle.'

Hermione breathed in the sweet air and noticed a brass plaque to the right of the front door that read:

"He who sees himself in all beings,
And all beings in him,
attains the highest Brahmin,
not by any other means"

Her father walked towards her dressed in a smart blue summer suit and uncharacteristic open-necked white shirt. He looked cheerful and relaxed.

'Darling, it's so lovely to see you. As you can see, the old factory is long gone, and we are now in a period of discovery. I want to have a long chat and, well, apologise for a lot of things. But enough of that for now, I spy a couple of rather financially well-endowed chaps that I must introduce myself to. See you later.'

He pecked her on the cheek and returned to the throng of business people.

Hermione stood watching the scene unfolding in front of her, *was it a dream, would she wake up any minute?*

As she twirled the invitation card in her hand, she noticed a small motif on the reverse.

The image of Ganesha.

18

Inside Outside

It's a strange feeling looking at them. I wonder if they mind – I don't suppose they do. Strangely, they look so lost; some smile and laugh, but the remainder walk around purposefully, with brows furrowed, deep in thought and overly focused as if to shut out the reality of life. Who knows what their problems are, they always look so anxious. They only have to ask or seek advice. I wonder why they don't. I feel sorry for them. I got to know a few over the last year; sadly, one or two have narrow minds and lack empathy, thought or consideration. Their views are often based on questionable logic and flawed, regimented social values.

So, I watch. I thought about this over the last months. At first, I felt guilty – as though I was intruding, but given my situation, I lost that sensitivity very quickly. Using a magazine or newspaper with a small hole in it, is effective but a bit obvious. I managed to put a small mirror to one side, and it worked really well because they thought I was looking the other way. I convinced myself that I observe out of genuine interest, not as a voyeur. But frankly, the way a number of them behave is actually quite laughable.

That approach was a bit of a faff, so I decided to just look at them directly – that is more honest. I am genuinely interested in how they tick – what are their values, what drives them, and what makes their hearts sing? Importantly, what makes them so different from me? Should I really feel sorry for them – do they feel sorry for me?

It is not easy to communicate with them. There is a reluctance to talk, or give away information – as if I would sell it to a newspaper or laugh at them – I ask you, how stupid is that?

Not all of them are fair and reasonable, one in particular is downright cruel. They use less physical violence these days, thank goodness. It is more a psychological sword that is brandished; the supercilious smile, which in itself is quite vicious given the circumstances between us. *Look at what I have, and you haven't...look at where I am going...look at where you're not going.* Or perhaps the allusion to what could happen to me if I continue to irritate. It's perhaps ironic, but I would not feel safe in the same space, not at all. Less safe because of the influence they have over everything.

I make notes, but I am not allowed to keep them because they are, so they say, an invasion of privacy. That makes me laugh. After all, they abuse my privacy without a second thought: the checks, removal of privileges, or lockdowns.

Frankly, I am happy to sit in this cell and look at those who walk up and down the walkways outside. They don't understand my life, the physical and sexual abuse at an early age, no education to speak of and the lack of money to provide for my young son; or all that I suffered before I made a stupid mistake and murdered the Post Office manager in a botched robbery – for which I genuinely weep.

Now I await the outcome of my appeal; an injection, or life in a cell, it's out of my hands.

For now, I just observe them.

19

Independence Day

Alan Roberts' parka did its best to prevent the autumn rain drip down his neck; it was only partially successful. This worsened his mood. He scuffed the brown leaves irritably as he walked along the path close to River Avon that flowed through the city of Bath, taking care not to stray too close to the edge. He knew all the walks in and around the ancient city, having memorised them from childhood. He rarely bumped into lamp posts or low walls now, painful experiences were etched on his shins.

Every time Alan walked down this path, he thought of carefree days of soft summer breezes and laughter for laughter's sake. Today he was using the walk to fight off a fit of mild depression, or as he termed it: serial grumpiness. He felt guilty about that. His life should have been ideal having met and married a woman who had been recently widowed quite young. Abigail was attractive and easy going, and their love was genuine, well-grounded, and mutually respectful. Alan worked freelance after leaving the editorship of a national magazine and this gave him the financial freedom they needed. Their finances were further strengthened by a legacy and Abigail was happy to give up work because she wanted more time to bring up their only child, a boy called Andy who was now in his early teens.

They sensibly reasoned that money isn't everything.

So, today Alan felt stupid as well as miserable. The problem was that Abigail did everything that associated with financial planning and making key family decisions; with his vision impairment worsening, this made sense. However, it did not sit easily with him. He felt marginalised and was beginning to resemble a character that was hard to please and moody.

Alan walked past the Bath Rugby Club to the bridge across the river Avon and joined North Parade Road, where he proceeded via various side roads to the city centre. The ball on his long cane clicked against the stony ground.

When he reached the site of the Roman Baths, he considered wandering about for a while, so walked left back into Stall Street with its quaint shops, some of them very old and others of more modern architectural design. He knew this to be just under a hundred metres long. It was beginning to get crowded with shoppers and he took care to hold his cane downwards, sweeping it slowly in an arc. Most people were courteous, others are not. He had grown used to dealing with all sorts of issues, but never gave ground or allowed any form of patronising or rudeness. That fact cut across his troublesome thoughts, and he stopped abruptly.

"Damnation, that's right. Nothing beats me, nothing," he mumbled angrily to himself. Just as he finished his outburst, he lost his balance, knocking into the corner of a building and yelped as he rebounded into someone. His. cane fell to the ground. and he stood, breathing heavily.

"I think you need to be cheered up," said a female voice with a strong foreign accent. "Here's your cane."

He reached out to the blurry image in front of him as the cane was put into his hands.

"Thanks, I'm fine, that's kind of you. I'm sorry I didn't see you," he said abruptly.

"I'm not surprised, my dear, my late husband said that sometimes I could be as quiet as a church mouse. In any case, your collision with the corner of the building didn't help. Look, I hope you don't take offence, but you look as though you need cheering up. It's my great age you know. Being over eighty, you can see everything in the world ever so clearly," adding, with a soft laugh, "then you spend the rest of your time wishing that you had known in your youth what you know now. Boy oh boy, what a time I would've had."

She let out a low, almost musical laugh, her accent was distinctly eastern European.

Alan's mood softened as he looked at her grey shape in the sunlight. "I'm not quite ancient, but I must say I'm beginning to feel a bit silly. The wall was immoveable, but to compensate, your personality is soothing, thank you."

Before he could say any more, she broke in.

"Okay, that settles it. I have you smiling already and so we agree that I am a tonic to anybody who feels a little sad. I have a small coffee shop just around the corner, perhaps you know it? It's called *Polka.*"

Alan shook his head and was about to demur when, unabashed, she continued almost without taking a breath. "Ah, you don't know it. Well, no matter. Shall we go there for coffee and cake, and you will then know where it is for future reference – it's on the house, of course."

Surprisingly, she knew exactly how to guide a visually impaired person. She put out her arm and before he could think twice, he found himself taking it and being guided rather than led. The coffee shop was a short distance away. Once inside, the richness of beans being roasted made his nose crinkle. The noise of the bean grinder and ensemble of coffee making machinery was almost too loud to allow conversation and Alan was guided to a table at the rear where it was surprisingly quiet. They sat in comfortable armchairs, designed to entice customers to stay longer.

"Forgive my bad manners, my name is Ellana Daskovitch. I am Polish and although the coffee comes from many parts of the world, in this coffee shop all the pastries are Polish." She gave an unseen smile and touched his hand.

"Well thank you, Ellana. My name is Alan Roberts and as you can see, I'm visually impaired. But don't let that fool you. I know every street in Bath and get around just fine. Thank you for guiding me to your coffee shop, you certainly knew how to do it properly. Sorry, I don't mean to patronise, but a lot of people don't have a clue."

"No offence taken, Alan, I assure you..."

"And please don't say how wonderful you think it is that someone *'like me'* can get around unaided," he snapped, almost too quickly.

"Ah, I see," she said, thoughtfully, "well for the record, Alan, I was not going to say that at all. In fact, I prefer that we ignore your sight loss and get on with important business."

"Oh?"

"Yes, very, very important. Picking the right pastry to celebrate your first time in my coffee shop," her voice rose musically.

Alan laughed at her theatrical manner and felt rather bad about snapping at her. He realised that he was prone to make too many snappy remarks these days and resolved to do something about it.

"Now then, I hope you don't mind, but I only have a small print menu so I will read it to you. Are you okay with that?"

"Only if you promise to produce some large print versions in future," he responded playfully.

"Yes, quite so, I promise. Here goes, you will like babka – it's called a grandmother cake and is rich and bread-like, often shaped like a woman's skirt, very cute and very tasty. Or perhaps you will like sernick, which is a kind of baked cheesecake. But my favourite, is szarlotka which is an apple and cinnamon cake, this is to Poles what apple pie is to Americans. I recommend it, it's delicious."

Ellana's gentle, good manners, and yet firm control of the environment she owned and knew well, made him feel comfortable in her company. He chose the szarlotka.

She was pleased with his choice and said, "Smakznego," explaining it meant "enjoy".

Alan finished the coffee and cake. The confused anxiety that dogged him had departed and he felt at ease, it was almost as though he had known her for years. There was a pause, and for reasons he could not explain he poured out his feelings.

Ellana touched his hand gently and said softly, "You have been lucky to find a woman who is worthy of your love and, from what you say loves you equally. You have a fine young boy, now eleven years old and no financial or other worries. Despite that, you feel miserable beyond all measure. Alan, it sounds a little selfish, if you don't mind me saying. If you were my son, I might be a little tough on you, you know that?"

Alan, put his hands together and looked up at the ceiling.

"Looking at it that way, Ellana, it does seem rather crass. But listen, it's not that I am ungrateful for my lot in life. It's just that deep in my heart there is a strong, energetic, creative, and independent being. I don't have any outlet for these impulses; in fact, I don't think I ever had. More than that, I know I am married to a lovely woman, and I do love her, really, I do, but I sometimes wonder if she loves me for who I am, or just as her 'blind bloke'?" When he finished, he screwed his face up, and Ellana was compelled to hold his hands tightly.

"That's a bit harsh on her, isn't it?" she said. "She is doing her best to be there for you in every way possible and you are resisting it. Is that fair?"

"Yes, I know I'm being unreasonable, but I want to jive, and she says I'll fall over, I want to sky-dive, but she thinks it would be dangerous," his voice rose slightly, and he placed both hands squarely on the table. "I yearn to do something completely different, a challenge perhaps, something that is mine and not given to me, I don't care how nutty it is. I want to be a free spirit, Ellana, can you understand that?"

Several older ladies sitting at nearby table looked up and Ellana half-turned to them smiling the kind of smile indicating, *everything is fine.*

Ellana turned back to Alan and said in a motherly tone, "Have you told your wife how you feel?"

Alan looked a bit sheepish. "Yes, well, I've tried, but she is so defensive and gets exasperated. She wants to know what more she can do and that's not the point, is it? It's not what she can do, but what I can do that counts. Does that make sense?"

Ellana thought for a moment. She waved her hand in a drinking motion to the shop assistant who brought a small bottle and two glasses. A ruby coloured liquid was then poured into the glasses, and she put one in his hand.

"Here, drink this. I promise that you will like it."

"What is it?"

She smiled. "Just drink it, Alan."

He swallowed it in one gulp and spluttered.

"Take it easy, dear man, this is my best plum brandy. I made it myself," she said feigning indignation. She took Alan's hands in her own and looked skywards for a brief moment, as if seeking spiritual guidance from her long-departed husband.

"Let me explain something to you. You know, your situation is no different from any other man's. For years I always supported my own dear husband in every way I could. I cherished him. He worked as a lorry driver and did hard manual labour, back in Poland, that is. Then I fell terribly ill and because I had no fallback position, he took time off and had to run my two coffee shops. Do you know what? He coped very well indeed. In fact, I had to admit the was better than me. We laughed about it, but in his own loving way he allowed me to take the reins again without any loss of pride on my part; but – and here's the point – he had proved himself. We were a different couple after that."

"So, what do I do, put something awful in my wife's coffee and run the home whilst she's sick?"

Ellana was halfway drinking her plum brandy and nearly spilled it, laughing aloud.

"Alan, I would definitely not do that. On the other hand, perhaps you just need to do something to wake her up." She leaned towards him as if to reinforce her message. "She's defending you like Mother Theresa, Alan, not shackling you. You must understand that."

They agreed to change the subject, drank two more plum brandies, and sat talking for a long while. Whilst they talked, he told her of his love of poetry and that he had written poems but didn't know what to do with them.

Ellana encouraged him to recite one that he had written after the break-up of his first relationship.

It all seems so amazing,
It's puzzling that for,
The fun goes out the window,
When you go out the door.

T'would take some understanding,
And I can tell you more,
A part of me is missing,
When you go out the door.

The only thing that I can think,
It shakes me to the core,
The best of me is absent,
Once you've gone out the door.

Ellana was enthralled and applauded loudly. Alan blushed and felt a little silly. As he turned away Ellana thought she could see a mist around him, choking his spirit. She looked up to the sky, more in hope of inspiration than anything else, and saw her imaginary muse, husband Gregory, shrugging, his hands in the air.

After they had finished their second cup of coffee, she decided to walk with Alan back to the High Street, not because he needed her help, but because it suited her to do so. She carefully put a half bottle of the plum brandy in a plastic bag and gave it to Alan to take home.

As they walked over the uneven paving stones, she described the shops they were passing, a new bookstore, a computer shop, and an art studio. Ellana stifled a laugh.

"And what are you laughing at, Mrs Daskovitch?" he said, amused.

"Oh, it's, well, it's a new art store and quite big, actually. They sell all sorts of equipment, and would you believe it they are advertising for models for their life classes?"

"Life classes?" he said slowly and quizzically.

"Yes, Alan, that means, models posing in the nude." Ellana sounded old fashioned, and he thought that she was even going to *tut tut*.

Alan stood for a while and Ellana didn't make a move to go. She was, after all, a guide, not a dog walker. He smiled broadly as he peered into the window of the art shop.

"Well, well, serendipity. Life class model, eh? That's different enough, isn't it?" he said turning to Ellana.

Her face dropped.

"Alan, I think my plum brandy was a little too strong for you. Shall we walk on now?"

Alan sensed her anxiety and enjoyed the unusual sense of power he exercised over her embarrassment.

He said, half playfully, "Let's go inside?"

She started to speak, but he cut her short, "You're not my keeper, Ellana, you can come in or go back to your coffee shop – what's it to be?"

Shrugging her shoulders, she resignedly guided him into the dimly lit shop, and they made their way through to the rear, past displays of canvasses, paints, brushes, and easels. The place smelled of linseed oil and turpentine – it was quite pleasant and yet different to other smells Alan was used to.

Ellana moved two curtains shrouding a central door and they entered a large studio. There was a desk on the left and a raised platform at the front of the room by a large window that opened onto a brick-walled courtyard. Between this and the curtains there were a dozen seats and easels set in a circle. To the left of the room a young woman stood cleaning an assortment of brushes. She was tall and slim with long ginger hair, and pleasant blue eyes. She looked up.

"Can I help you? I'm Christine Thompson, I teach art here."

Ellana stood to one side open-mouthed and listened as Alan negotiated the going rate for posing as an artists' model. She felt helpless.

She heard the teacher explaining the work and that it only paid eight pounds fifty pence an hour. Alan talked to the teacher who listened to her for a while then laughed.

"Okay, Alan, so you don't think you are in the best of shape, well from where I'm standing you look great. But you are making a big mistake. We like people just as they are thanks, we're not after magazine models or Mr Universe, just someone who can sit still and be painted just as they are. Is that clear? I'll give you a proper brief so turn up about twenty minutes early."

They shook hands and Alan joined Ellana. Together they left the studio. He explained that he agreed to attend on a couple of future dates, the first session was next Wednesday at eleven o'clock in the morning and had promised not to let the teacher down. As he outlined the situation in detail, realisation set in, and he started to get nervous; the full ramifications of what he had agreed to do came home to him.

He had actually agreed to take off all his clothes and sit in front of twelve complete strangers for two hours. Alan Roberts, who wore a vest and pyjamas and never changed into swimming shorts on the beach!

Ellana noticed that he was slightly flushed and when they were outside the shop said, "I'm sorry to ask, but are you sure about this?"

Quick as a flash, the old Alan stubbornness came to the fore.

"Ellana, I am quite sure, really I am, I know my own mind, you know. *Something different* we said, well, shockingly different will do then," he stated with new found conviction.

Ellana looked up at the sky and again sought spiritual guidance from Gregory, but all she could conjure up in her mind was his admonishing gaze and shaking head.

"I suppose it is, Alan, I suppose it is."

They turned and walked in silence to the High Street. When they got there Ellana wished him well and hoped that everything would work out. Alan pecked her on the cheek and, ignoring the butterflies in his stomach that were now sailing in gale force ten, thanked her for her kindness and generosity. He turned and headed home, identifying various "markers" along the way, matching them with his rehearsed route in his mind.

Alan knew that his moods had been affecting Abigail and son Andy and resolved to put things right. When he arrived home, he made cheerful small talk whilst she prepared the evening meal and asked them both how their respective days had gone. They didn't ask about his day, but then why should they? For all they knew it would be his usual perambulation from the newsagents to shops and then home. If they had asked, he would have told them about meeting the lovely Ellana, her pastries and plum brandy, and of course, his new job.

The weekend came and went and before he knew it, it was Monday, and he thought about tomorrow, which was "D-Day". Abigail busied herself with housework and the house sparkled. She cleaned everything in sight, baked cakes, prepared pot-roast, did the ironing and organised a plumber to fix the shower, before settling down to do the family accounts. Alan sat at his computer and felt like a spare part.

Andy turned to his mum. "Is dad okay, mum?"

Abigail calmed him. "Yeah, yeah, he's just over-tired. Now then, look at the lovely cakes, let's damage a few?"

They both tucked into the baking and made appreciative remarks between mouthfuls of dough. Alan heard and took a deep breath, then put his head around the door and said, "What's this then, pig trough time?" playfully wagging a finger and smiling.

"Come on in, eat as many as you like, they'll only go stale after, um, let's see, seven and a half minutes."

Alan playfully barged to towards the plate.

Andy laughed, "My gosh, dad, one minute gone already, we'd better go some." Laughing, they reached for more, both fighting for the one with the chocolate topping.

Alan withdrew, shouting that he was going for a bath. It made him smile to see them so happy. They rarely argued and he knew how lucky he was, which made him stop halfway up the stairs. Was he being stupid? Then he remembered that during his talk with Ellana, it had become clear that he had to do something to step outside his circle of dependency, to do something to gain a foothold on a life where at present he felt that he was only a resentful bystander.

As the bath filled, steaming the room, and foaming the water, Alan tried to make out his body in the large mirror above the sink. He squinted but his central vision was quite poor. Turning on the overhead lights made little difference. He could make out a shape, but how could he tell whether or not it was okay? He flexed his muscles, remembering his fit and lithe body of a decade or so ago. When he heard the sound of two pairs of feet thumping up the stairs he quickly hopped into the bath.

"Yeeeow," he cried and hopped out again; his feet were red four inches past his ankle. "Blast and damn!"

Abigail looked in. "Well, Mr Handsome, lovely bum by the way. I presume you burned your tootsies!"

With one hand Alan turned the cold tap on and the other he threw a wet sponge at her as she left. Once in the bath, he used its calming warmth to relax himself and practise visualisation, it always worked.

He went into a calm half-sleep in the warm and softened water, and visualised positive images to reinforce confidence and push out the negative thoughts. A scene too shape of him walking into the studio. The room was full of faceless people and they all warmly welcomed him. He felt at ease in their company. One woman explained how she could never pose in the nude and that Alan was so brave. This made him feel good, he was doing something that someone else could not even contemplate. Then he was on the plinth and Christine Thompson was introducing him in a matter-of-fact way, turning to the audience saying...

"Darling, have you seen the toothpaste?" Abigail's voice broke the spell. He sat bolt upright in the bath, bubbles on his nose and eyes wide open and saw her standing by the sink waving a toothbrush.

"Crikey, you look just like a baby seal, big eyes and a snowy foam all over your nose."

He laughed. "You crackpot," he said, "I was half asleep."

"Hmmm. Half asleep huh? Well, perhaps you need awakening?" Her left hand deftly drew the lock across the bathroom door, and she knelt by the bath, her hand slowly moving into the warm water. She kissed him gently on the cheek. Submission was the perfect antidote to his mood.

The next morning Alan felt groggy through lack of sleep. He slept fitfully throughout the night, duelling with a multiplicity of demons. In his half-sleep he saw that the artists in the studio included two of Andy's friends with the inevitable mobile phone cameras, his father-in-law sat with his arms folded and his mother-in-law leaned forward with her mouth wide open. The bank manager was there and so was his neighbour, Joan Rushby, who kept saying, "Ooh, really," and putting her hand to her mouth.

After Andy had gone to school and he had eaten a solitary breakfast, Alan remembered that he had put the plum brandy that Ellana had given him into the food cupboard. Abigail put on her coat, kissed him gently and went on her weekly shopping trip. She would be out during the morning, and it gave him the opportunity to retrieve the elixir – that would steady his nerves. He poured the thick rich liquid into a small glass and before he knew it, he swallowed three more glasses of brandy to gain courage. It made his eyes glaze and his blood race. No wonder they used to give soldiers a tot of spirit before going into battle.

It was ten o'clock and his heart skipped a beat. Only one more hour to go. He decided to take the plum brandy with him to the studio and put the bottle into a shopping bag, then gathered up his parka and gloves. He was so nervous he could hardly remember the way into town. But once outside the house and on his way, confidence returned, or at least some of it, and he made it safely to the studio without a problem.

However, as he stood outside the door, his heartbeat increased, and he felt giddy and a little anxious. "Just one more tot," he thought, but inevitably took three good swallows. Zip, that was good. Then he took one more slug for luck. Zip, that was good too. In fact, it was so good he found himself laughing. Who cares, - everyone is born naked, so what's the big deal? I wonder what Christine Thompson looks like in the buff. He took yet another swig, oblivious of the looks from passers-by. Licking his lips, he dispensed with the bottle, now empty, into the paper bag and put it against the wall of the studio.

"Okay, this it is, or, should I say, 'is it'," and stifled a nervous giggle.

Alan had been brave all his life, he had to be to survive. Today was no different. Pulling himself up straight he marched, a little unsteadily, into the shop and through to the studio. He tipped two easels over and spilled the brushes, before finally stopping at the curtains that shrouded the entrance to the main studio. His heart thumped with dread.

"Okay, okay, let's do it," he whispered to himself determinedly and with a whisk of his hands opened the curtains and squinted into the studio. The smell of linseed oil and turpentine was in the air and the room was warm and strangely quiet. He squinted and saw shapes at the easels and a figure at the front, which he surmised, must be the teacher, Christine Thompson.

Alan walked forward unsteadily, dropping his parka to the floor as he went. "Hello everybiddy, everybody, sorry."

He slipped off his white polo shirt and nonchalantly threw it over an easel. Equally as deftly, he undid his belt and his jeans dropped to the ground. He kicked them to one side as he walked, along with his slip-on shoes and finally paused and he put his thumbs into his underpants.

"It was the triffic, sorry traffic, not that I drive, no not me, hic, because I'm visually implored, I mean impaired." He looked down at his hands and steeled himself for the final drop as his thumbs gripped the elastic. "Oops, sorry, I'm not used to this."

"Alan, stop, for goodness sake stop!" a voice shouted.

It was Christine Thompson. She came towards him, and the light faded momentarily as a sheet was lifted high then wrapped gently around him.

"Alan, you chump, are you by any chance a little pickled?"

He was guided to a seat and sat down gratefully.

"Alan, I don't need you today, our life class session is tomorrow, Wednesday, today is Tuesday. I did tell you." She paused and looked around her. "Perhaps you can't quite make it out, but each of the chairs is heaped with canvas covers, not students. Thank goodness we are alone. And whilst we are at it, my beefy striptease dancer, we don't get our models to sashay along the aisle casting their clothes left and right. Models have a changing cubicle and a robe to wear until its class time. Then they go to the plinth and the robe is removed. It's about professional dignity and respect. No comments about your physique are tolerated and, not that I suspect you would, no fraternising either way."

She leaned forward and said gently, "Now then, if the cleaning lady caught you in your undies and me standing here wide-eyed, I don't think that would be any good for my reputation, do you?"

Alan squinted at her, then let out a large, "Hic," and they both burst out laughing.

"Oh, dear, Christine, I feel such a flipping pillock. I was so nervous, and I just had one or six too many brandies. I just have one more big problem," he said.

"Oh, what's that?"

"Well, Christine. I don't think I will be able to find my clothes."

They laughed some more, and Christine returned them to him and left him to get dressed in private. Then she made a coffee and reassured him about the correct process of being a life class model.

"There's a knack to it," she said, calmly but with a hint of a smile. "You really must keep completely detached from the class and not make eye contact with the artists. The art of keeping as still as possible involves focusing directly on something at the back of the room and breathing slowly - but definitely don't look at people in front of you because it will distract you and you'll move."

"Okay, I'll remember that. But what exactly do you want me to do?"

"We have various angles that I can get you to pose in, basically you will do four fifteen-minute poses in various positions like reaching up or kneeling, perhaps even holding a vase or something, then one hour in a fixed position which is usually reclining on a couch. Don't worry, I shan't get you to hold a cactus!"

Alan laughed but was nonetheless grateful for that.

"One last thing. You can wander around the studio and talk to artists at the break - in a robe of course - and view their work. Do please stay after the full session to talk. However, avoid making comments on the sketches, frankly some will be quite awful, but we're not here to judge, rather to encourage. Sessions are strictly timed for two hours, no more."

Christine's briefing was straightforward and uncomplicated. All Alan had to do was turn up – and strip off!

The next day, to Alan's surprise, he was full of confidence. There was certainly more to this than just getting your kit off. Besides, nothing could be as embarrassing as his faux pas the day before. True to her word Christine showed him to the changing cubicle and he made himself ready for the class, changing into a silk robe. She guided him to the front, and he was introduced to each of the students, and with his approval, she explained his visual impairment to them. It was interesting listening to her brief the class on what she expected to see from their life class drawings, the emphasis on the muscles and shading and so on.

Before he knew it, he was on the plinth, seated comfortably on a small soft stool. Christine asked him to remove the robe by just letting it slide off and he did so quickly and without fuss.

That was it. He was quite naked.

His first pose involved holding a shield and large spear. He liked that and cheerfully thought that if perchance anyone made a rude comment, he could see them off!

All he could hear was the frantic scratching of charcoal and pencil against cartridge paper. No heavy breathing, no "Ooh really," from anyone, no gasps, just scratching. More short poses followed and true to Christine's brief, he ended up posing face down on a couch, arching his back and resting his head in his hands

As time went on, he felt a little exhilarated. He was doing something that probably only one in a hundred people would do. A cool draft wafted across his body, and he actually felt good being naked. He had to admit that there was just a small tinge of excitement or naughtiness, but instinctively knew that the more times he did it the more this would fade so he would gather the feeling up whilst it lasted.

One particular student at the back of the class needed guidance. Ellana sat wide-eyed and hardly drawing at all. She started unsteadily to draw a figure. After fifteen minutes she was nudged and her neighbour said softly, "Er, Ellana, isn't it? You need to use my rubber. It's the right breast on your drawing, ma'am. It's got two nipples."

Ellana gasped, blushed, and took the rubber to quickly rub out the offending circle. Behind her, a girl let out a quiet giggle. She left before the end of the session.

The class finished and Alan dressed. Christine gave him coffee and seventeen pounds in cash. It felt good. He couldn't see the way people were looking at him, but from the tone of their voices they seemed to like him and in no way treated him differently from anyone else. Some of them were interested in his eye condition, but most of all they were talking to him because of the help he had given them – just by modelling. It was such a good feeling – they wanted to talk to him. They valued him.

Before he left Christine said, "Alan, you were really very good. You have a nice body, very nice indeed in fact, but you kept so still, which is really difficult, it makes it so good for the artists. You are a natural. That said, I am so very grateful you left off the plum brandy today."

Alan prodded her playfully with his cane. She was easy to talk to and he told her how he felt today.

"Alan, it is really all about art, but we wouldn't be human if we didn't feel a bit funny the first time around. Just think yourself lucky you're not like the younger male model we had in the other day. He will remember his first time, because, how shall I say this, his embarrassment was obvious for all to see if you get my drift."

Alan laughed. "Oh dear, poor chap!"

He stayed a while longer and they talked about art and poetry, and before he knew it, he had to dash home for supper. It had been a good day and he felt confident and positive.

Alan continued posing for three months and was a new man at home and with friends. Everyone had noticed the change in him. Then one day he returned from the life class to find Abigail sitting in the lounge. As he came in Andy joined them.

"Hello, you're home early?"

"Er, yes," said Abigail quizzically, "I have a strange question for you. Alan, Andy said that he, well, he and his friends that is, saw an oil painting. It was, well, it was of you in the nude."

Alan felt her embarrassment but was unfazed.

"Have you seen it?"

"Well, yes, I have," she replied nervously.

"And did you like it?"

Abigail thought for a moment, "Well, I ..."

"Abigail, did – you – like – it?"

Before she could answer, Andy intervened. "My friends said you have great pecs, dad."

Abigail cuffed Andy and Alan intervened.

"Well, thank them for me, dear boy. In fact, thank you for passing the comment on. Do you know something? That's the first time anyone has paid me a compliment in this house for more years than I can remember. You want to know how I yearn to be told something positive, something other than 'hi dad', or 'you look tired dad.' Do you know how much I ache to have you compliment me on something substantial? Think about that."

Alan felt bad about saying that and was red-faced and retreated to his study. Abigail looked sheepish as the penny began to drop. It was their way never to trespass on each other's feelings, preferring to let time smooth the differences. She got up to make a pot of tea. Later, neither of them felt any immediate need to talk further on the subject, but she did gently touch his shoulder a few times.

Abigail carefully thought about what Alan said and the next day she skipped work and went to the art studio. She stood outside looking in the window at the oil painting of Alan in a nude pose. She had to admit that he looked stunning. Not just good, but bloody stunning. After a while, a long while, she became aware of someone standing next to her. It was an older woman.

"He's lovely, isn't he? Such a good build and so very handsome."

"Yes, he is. He's my husband."

"Ah!" said the woman. "It must be like looking at him from a different angle or perhaps with a different pair of spectacles on? Do you see a different person perhaps? Let me introduce myself, my name is Ellana Daskovitch, and you must be Abigail?"

"Why yes, but how...?"

"Never mind, Abigail, never mind. Would you like a cup of coffee from my lovely Polish coffee shop? I would like to talk to you."

Bemused, Abigail agreed and together they made their way down the street to the shop. When they were seated, Ellana explained how she had met Alan. She hated breaking a habit of a lifetime and confided Alan's private fears to Abigail. She hoped for the best. She breathed a sigh of relief when it became clear that Abigail was motivated to know more and work out a solution to help her man. Then they talked more. Ellana, the older woman with a lifetime's experiences and Abigail, the reserved English rose, who needed as much advice as Alan did. After further conversation, a bright idea emerged; it must have been the plum brandy that lubricated the senses. Abigail smiled and addressed Ellana enthusiastically.

"Yes, by golly, I think that's a great idea, I'll do it."

She stood up straight, took a deep breath, hugged Ellana and left the coffee shop. They parted, now firm friends. Ellana looked up at the sky at Gregory's spiritual image, and imagined him splaying his hands left and right, looking hopeless, as if to say, *what have you done?* She frowned at him dismissively.

"Okay, what more can I do? I didn't tell her I fancied him though, Gregory, he is such a kind man and so good looking. I hope you forgive me?"

She raised a glass of plum brandy and smiled broadly. "Besides, I am too old and still think of you, my love."

Looking through the window to the far side of the street, she saw Abigail standing outside the art studio before eventually going inside. She smiled broadly.

"So, she did listen to what I said."

Family Roberts made it through the rest of the week without incident. Neither Alan nor Abigail felt it necessary to get upset and when Friday came Abigail produced two bottles of red wine and they settled down to talk. Before they knew it, they had talked for hours and eventually fell asleep. They awoke on the couch early on Saturday morning. Andy stayed with friends for the weekend, so they had the house to themselves. They talked more than they had ever done, and it felt good to get things off their chests. Abigail listened to all that was said – that Ellana was a clever lady.

She wasn't upset when Alan told her that he'd written poetry but did gently remonstrate with him for not showing it to her. She read them and told him how good they were, then gently asked him never to keep such things to himself again – they must share everything in future. There was a tinge of regret, but she knew that she had to change her attitude towards Alan. However, she also had plans of her own.

The rest of the weekend continued in the same vein, lying in each other's arms listening to countless long-playing records that had lain unheard for years and making love as much as nature would allow. It was perfectly sublime.

When Alan got home on the Wednesday after his studio work, he heard Andy in the lounge giggling and laughing and Abigail was trying to silence him with whispers and threats. Abigail came to the lounge door and smiled; it was a kind of wan smile that partners make when they've bought an expensive item on the overdraft and are still thinking about the right words to use to explain.

"Hello darling, you're early," she said, clasping her hands in front of her.

"Not really, and you're acting very strangely, what is it?" he replied with a crooked smile.

Andy laughed and rolled on the couch holding his stomach. Abigail cast him a "be quiet" look.

"I, er, need to show you something darling, well, 'show and tell' really, if you get my drift."

"No," Alan said, puzzled. He entered the lounge and at first didn't notice anything. "Do make sense, Abigail."

"First the 'tell', I've got a job. Part time, that's all."

Alan looked at her aghast and before he could say anything she added, "Don't argue, the mortgage is paid off and frankly I'm due for a change in my life. It's a bit of freelance accounting. The extra cash will enable us to, well, have some fun. Yes, that's it, fun!"

Alan sat down on the arm of the couch. He was speechless.

"Another thing, I, well, I want you to accept a gift. It's a painting."

Andy stuffed a handkerchief in his mouth to stop him laughing.

Abigail said nervously, "I hope you like it."

She guided Alan to the far wall of the room and as he drew closer to a painting, he smelled the familiar warm smell of linseed oil and turpentine. Alan reached for his magnifier, opened it up and walked to the large oblong shape on the wall and Abigail bent the reading light so that it shone onto the picture.

After scanning the painting, he stopped in the middle.

"Is that," he said as he got closer, "my goodness it is, it's— ooh, Abigail, is it you?"

Abigail smiled like a twelve-year-old who has just baked her first scone.

"Yup, it's me. Do you like it? And while we're at it please look at *all* the painting, young man."

Alan looked at her lovingly. "Yes, yes, I really like it. And may I add, not bad for a woman of your age."

That was enough for Andy, and he made an "urgh" sound and dashed to the kitchen.

They embraced and held each other in a lingering kiss. Alan gazed at Abigail. "But why you in the nude. Why, you chump?"

"Because I need to be a free spirit too, Alan, don't you understand? I needed to do the same thing as you. You succeeded. You showed me what to do. If it meant shedding inhibitions and doing a bit more listening, then so be it. Well done. Thank you darling."

Alan's eyes moistened, but he had no time to indulge in sentiment. The doorbell rang and Andy popped his head around the door.

"Tell him mum, tell him, quick."

"There's more?" said Alan.

"Yes, there is. The person Andy is letting in is called Jim Novak. He's a literary agent. Anyway, you did give me your poems to read, and I showed them to him. I hope you don't mind. He's really excited, Alan, and wants to work with you. Here's the good bit. Jim's confident that he has a publisher for your work and wants you to do more. How about that?"

Alan sat down again, bemused, overjoyed and for a moment short of words. He stood up abruptly as a thought occurred to him. "Goodness, Abigail, cover the picture up, quickly, before he comes into the room."

Abigail smiled at him. "Oh, that's okay, he was in the life class I modelled for, and it's his painting."

Alan yelped and fell back onto the couch.

20

Why?

My family told me not to do it, but I had no choice. No work, no money and my mates were committed – so I did. My parents cried and, for that matter, so did I. Despite the danger I was putting myself in, I saw that they were proud of me. I suddenly felt like a man, as if I had grown another six centimetres. I waved my family goodbye and told them I would return a hero. I was going to make a difference. They smiled and laughed weakly at my childish self-belief. I knew it was only words, and so did they.

I stuck my chest out and felt part of a group of comrades, all of us standing shoulder to shoulder. We underwent the usual checks and basic preparation. The battlefield training was done later in the arid landscapes that mirrored our eventual deployment and was unforgivingly tough, but I worked hard and reached the required standard. The real thing would be different – I knew that.

Some of my comrades are very strange, they come from all walks of life. Most of us are committed and have a sense of balance between right and wrong, but a few of them are different, more bellicose and itching for a fight, and quite cruel when they can get away with it - which is why they joined. That is what conflict encourages: men acting like animals, doing bad things just because they can. The further they get from authority and accountability the worse they become. These are men that I would have talked with as friends outside this conflict. Men who have families and kiss their children. Men who stroke their cats and love their grandparents. Men who now kill happily without a second thought and without mercy.

Once into the conflict, tension rises. A mission has to be completed according to orders and directions; discipline is crucial. However, when the first shot is fired it all changes, a bit like a game of chess. The first move causes the next and the next, and the first death causes rage, then retribution, then more death, and after that there is no turning back. Planning – shouting – confusion – surprise – retaliation. It has been the same since ancient times and nothing changes.

I wonder why the enemy do what they do to incur our anger. Surely it doesn't have to be this way. The dead pile up: old men, women and children who did nothing wrong in their lives, simply labelled collateral damage. All that crying and anger. There are no friends anywhere – not now anyway. I know that local people do not know whom to befriend, they just want to live and get on with their lives. I weep for them. But all I can do is reload my weapon and fire at the enemy. No prisoners. If they take us then we can expect no quarter, so we respond the same way. Besides, who will judge us, here in the rocks and sand of Helmand? We must remain focused; there is no room for hesitation.

I see his face. He is young and about my age. I do not hate him, but he is my enemy. He holds his rifle to one side as he gazes at an aircraft circling in the sky above the devastation of what was used to be a school. He picks up a child's bloodied shoe, grimaces and then throws it down. I can see that he is angry, and he shouts abuse at the aircraft. I feel his confused anger too but have no choice.

His head is clear in the crosshair sight on my rifle, and I slowly squeeze the trigger. He falls. I do not shout with joy. I just breathe deeply and hope that his God will accept him into heaven after questions about how he has led his life. If I fall in the same way I hope I will also be forgiven all my sins.

I do not want these men here and so I must fight them.

Allah will forgive me – I know he will.

21

Enlightenment

Anger needs to be controlled. Violence needs to be managed. When both characteristics are out of control, all sensibility is lost, compassion dies, and chaos ensues. Peter knew this well enough.

He had been angry, very angry in Sierra Leone, but maintained his discipline - until the right time. When the perpetrators of child rape and murder were cornered, that time arrived. They contemptuously threw down their arms, advancing with smiles, expecting Geneva Convention mercy that they knew would lead to respite, then rehabilitation and freedom to return to the old ways at a later date to create more misery.

The smiling mouths full of white teeth, and the swaggering, soon changed to disbelief and painful grimaces as bullets ripped into their flesh.

Peter cared little for the lives of guerrillas who conveniently masqueraded behind dubious ideologies that destroyed fellow human beings without conscience. He was reminded of Shakespeare's play, Timon of Athens in which two senators discuss the fate of a captain under sentence of death, postulating that, *nothing emboldens sin so much as mercy.*

The bush is a quiet place, solitary, away from the eyes of third parties who see the world from a notebook, wringing their liberal hands, detached from the searing reality of conflict.

However, times change, endless observation and press reporting intervenes. Liberals meant well, but lofty principles always come at a price. Peter believed in his own sense of right and wrong, and that checks and balances were needed to stop people on all sides of conflict doing evil things. Above all, mercy must be balanced by justice – but sometimes the definition or understanding of justice was vacant or confused.

It was Bosnia that eventually killed his spirit. Official Rules of Engagement forbade UN soldiers from intervening, even when young Muslim drivers were hauled from trucks by Serb militia and shot right in front of blue-bereted soldiers; peacekeeping is different from peace-making. Iraq and Afghanistan underscored the dichotomy between these rules and the red mist of battle, never fully understood in the sterile, wooden-clad courtrooms of Europe.

Peter stood six feet in his socks, toned and muscular even though he was now past his late forties. His hair was cropped short, and his face had angular features. Deep blue eyes gave him a formidable appearance. It made him memorable. He was noticed. He was never ignored. Aware of this, he tried to smile broadly when the occasion demanded to redress the stern image. When he did, the sun shone.

He looked across at the only small window to his whitewashed room. It was simply furnished and smelled of sandalwood, a paradise compared to the horrors of Helmand. His rehabilitation had been effective. Alcohol dependence was a thing of the past and his personal discipline returned, stronger than ever. Now he had purpose to add to his personal standards of justice. He knew that not many people would share them, but that was what made him special. Nonetheless, he held on tightly to the notion that anger, and violence were sometimes necessary in a world in which evil people lived; however, it was discipline and control that provided the necessary brakes on what, how and when to do anything.

His school days had shown him that any sign of being gentle or weak led to verbal or physical abuse. He made it his mission to avoid that consequence. It was common sense, after all. Mental balance and what his late father called "the right action at the right time" was the key to success. That was the blunt truth of it all.

Here he was, back in uniform, different and with a new doctrine to adhere to, but in his case not to be a slave to it. He respected and followed its values and direction, recognising the all-important ingredients of social structure and rules to guide people and avoid badness; it was a necessary prop for mankind. However, he was his own man within this ancient institution and was known for his particular interpretation of how to deal with evil things that so confused his peers.

When he heard of a colleague who had abused young boys, he didn't wring his hands - he used them. The punishment he dealt out was severe. The man was ordered to report to the police and confess, lest it be repeated, often. Of course, it would be considered unbelievable for a man in his position, if it became known, but he cared not. Not for him the suffocating excuses and dithering, often evident in such situations.

When he became aware of wife-beating, rape, or robbery from the elderly, he dealt with things in his own personal way.

It is difficult to punish with a kind heart and moderate persona, but equally, Peter knew he had to balance anger and violence. Proper corroboration was, of course, necessary. He always had to be sure of a situation.

His superiors were perplexed, sometimes nervous and yet accepted that he was a maverick who achieved results. They felt awkward, but knew his heart was stout and true. Nevertheless, they resigned themselves to the fact that if matters became challenging, they would have to turn away from him and claim ignorance.

Peter's new uniform was less pugnacious, comforting to the mild, but a barrier to the violent and arrogant and, in his case, camouflaging steely retribution.

News soon spread. He became the protector, a comforter to those less equipped to deal with bad things. When he spoke to people, he didn't just feel their pain, he mirrored their mood. He encouraged love and compassion. Equally, he was the nemesis to evil doers.

The early morning sunlight shone on to the crucifix above his bed and it made him feel calm at the beginning of his day. Today, he would be helping a grieving widow and later would be talking to children in a local orphanage.

He felt a little strange in his long black gown with its white tab collarless shirt. He put his round black four-cornered berita hat on and smiled regarding it all as necessary props, for a necessary mission.

As he turned to leave his room, he reached to the bookcase and flipped open a dog-eared leather notebook. On the facing page he had written:

Bene esse fortissimum
(To do good you must be strong...)

22

The Journey

Clickety-clack, along the track. That's what we used to say when we travelled on this train, all those years ago. Travelling in anything other than first class used to be unacceptable, unbearable; but now things are different – so be it. Clickety-clack, the whole family would sing as we travelled, food would be served, wine poured, and we laughed. It is true that we were privileged; that was then.

In those days crying children were sent to the back of the train and anyone badly dressed was also asked to leave the carriage and move further back; no chance of that now. No seat reservation, no discipline and certainly no choice.

Despite everything, it is odd that the joy of travelling to a large city remains the same – for different reasons now, but nevertheless, just the same; the anticipation and longing to be at the destination now understandably stronger. Clickety-clack, that hypnotising, repetitive sound that blocks out background noise allowing the miles to be eaten up almost unaccountably as the mind is lulled and, oh, how the mind needs to be lulled. Do the best you can to block out everything but the thought of arrival. Block it out.

Clickety-clack, that friendly track, that takes me now, as it used to do, to a place of comfort and sanctuary, away from the confusion that envelops me, promising to leave chaos far behind. I remember how wonderful it was to get away from the frantic pressure of financial markets or property deals, or even quarrelsome family or friends, minds full of selfish trivia, bent on the pursuit of one-upmanship, or greed. It was simple, a short break to refuel the senses before returning refreshed.

Not now, perhaps not ever.

Clickety-clack – is it only me that focuses on this? Will they never stop pushing four people to seats made for two and allowing the children to wail so loudly? Is there no guard or inspector? Where is the refreshment? Some water at least? Never mind. Clickety-clack, block it out with the dull repetition of track rattle, broken in cadence only when new or broken rails are traversed. It's all the same.

Suddenly it stops. Everything is quiet.

We disembark.

The air is thick with expectation, cleaving to every single person. Expectation, that screams: let it be better.

There is something oddly comforting to be amongst people who speak a different tongue – one hears nothing of interest and even the nuances of speech are lost; how wonderful, not to hear bad language, insults, or threats. Bliss. No thumping heart or tight chest at the turmoil around or having to make excuses to avoid a harsh shout or demand, pretending to be ignorant of the challenge, but so very aware of the danger. Now, no head down, but head up; smile and be thankful – be anything but afraid.

The line is long, and the time taken to reach the end is also mind-numbingly lengthy, but no matter, we are here, all equal in our misery and equal in our quest. At last, here, where horrific murder and rape are not a daily occurrence, and a uniform or mode of dress does not engender electrifying fear.

No clickety-clack now, just the tip-tap of heels as they walk slowly along the platform towards a single desk in a large steel shed masquerading as a hotel reception.

I always loved Vienna, but now it embraces me in a different way.

Things change.

23

Quick Thinking

Columbia is beautiful - today it had a different shine. Brother Jim said it was a dodgy place, as usual I disagreed.

We sat on a damp mossy log at the side of a ragged trail that led through the Choco-Darien rain forest. Leaning unsteadily against a tree, was a man dressed in an amusing mix of Nike sports shorts and combat jacket. His unkempt hair and beard made him look like a mad, comical character in the Muppet Show; he was anything but amusing. He gripped an AK47 rifle in his left hand and hurriedly searched our wallets and rucksacks with his other.

Jim gave me a *told you so* look. He put his hand on my shoulder, reassuringly, but without conviction. 'Peter, he's spaced out.'

'*Callete*,' shouted the gunman angrily, pointing his rifle menacingly at Jim; his bloodshot gaze was terrifying.

Jim bridled. 'Rude bastard, my Spanish says that's shut up!'

The gunman's agitation increased, '*Oye, billetes*...er, dollars, eh?' He gestured to his trousers. We demonstrated our lack of cash by standing and pulling out the insides of our pockets, splaying our empty hands to our sides.

He shrugged, picked at a red spot on his neck and gave a twisted smile at Jim. 'Okayee. You are dead, eh?'

I needed to think fast. As his finger closed over the trigger, I screamed, 'No!'

The gunman recoiled, smirking. He reached into his trousers and brought out a bottle of greyish-brown spirit, removed the cork with his teeth, spat it out and took a large swig.

I theatrically opened my shirt, banged my chest, and searched for basic Spanish. 'That's not fair - him, my brother, *hermano,* always first*, siempre primero. Yo primero,* me first....!'

The gunman looked bemused, shook his head slowly, and took another swig. As he resignedly turned the rifle towards me, Jim shouted, 'Stop!' He feigned anger, dismissively pointing at me. '*Hermano idiota.* No, no, no... *Yo primero!*'

The gunman's face twisted in confusion, and he hunched over and took another swig of spirit. Staggering, he revolved his index finger against his forehead and muttered, '*Loco!*' and repeatedly moved the rifle first to Jim then me, grinning as he taunted us, laughing raggedly. Then he put his head back and drank deeply.

Too deeply.

Jim launched himself forward and smacked the base of the bottle. The gunman gagged as it filled his throat. The rifle fell to the ground and went off with a loud crack.

As we tidied out rucksacks, Jim pointed to a large Condor that had been watching us from the forest canopy. 'He was hoping for lunch,' he said. I shuddered at the thought.

The gunman looked forlorn tied to a tree and wriggled against his bonds. I wagged my finger at him. '*Ahora callete,* now you shut up! ' Pointing to the road I said angrily, '*La policia...!*'

As we walked away, and Jim turned to me. 'I don't always get my own way.'

'Do!'

'Don't.'

'Do...you bloody do!'

'Idiota...!'

24

Hubris

I smirk, what a slick charmer I am. I spray aftershave, put on my gold chain, and trim my moustache, then drive off in my aged MG Midget. I park and call a girlfriend I dated over twenty years ago. I gaze at her sitting outside a café, looking as lovely as ever. I could hardly hold the mobile as I dialled. We talk about bygone days. We laugh. We bond. She enthusiastically says we must meet up. Suddenly, alarmed, she gets up. 'Sorry, Jack. Call again. Gotta go. There's a creepy old pervert staring at me from an MG.'

Printed by Amazon Italia Logistica S.r.l.
Torrazza Piemonte (TO), Italy

41646085R00107